Bittersweet Tears

By

L.J. Newlin

Reader Advisory

This novel contains strong language and violence. It is intended for adult reading.

Dedication

To my Husband Doug, who lovingly supports my artistic quests. To my sons, Jeremy and Ryan who taught me the joys of motherhood. To my father Donald Gustafson, whose death provoked a deep need to express my heart felt emotions in writing and in painting. I thank God that you all have been a very special part of my life.

Acknowledgements

Spanish translation supplied by my friend, Juan Alvarado.

A special thanks to Frank and Sandy Ellis, whose help with the editing was a gift from god.

Contents

Introduction

Poem

Chapters

Introduction

Laura Daniels is an attractive woman in her early forties, widowed with two sons. She is an opinionated, strong willed individual who has a vast capacity to care and love. She had put her life on hold since her husband's death, dedicating all her energies to raising her boys, Matt and Kyle. She had always done her best, but at times, her best seemed damned ugly. Laura felt she was a failure when it came to her youngest, and that caused much anguish in her heart. She had acquiesced to a life of being alone, unmarried, until she met Dave.

David Martin, a divorcee had also chosen to postpone the pursuit of a life's partner, until his daughters had left the nest. He was a man of character, integrity, and strength. Dave was a passionate man, full of life and love. He brought more into people's lives than he ever took. His daughters had always been the center of his universe. Then by chance, luck, or God's intervention he met Laura. He knew the first time they talked she was a woman worth pursuing. It was from that moment on their lives were intricately intertwined.

As a moth is attracted to light, so also is evil attracted to good. From the very first time Dave and Laura met, evil had interjected itself into their lives. For the most part, they were unaware of the foreboding cloud, which hung over their lives and what ultimate destruction and pain it would cause. This evil was in the form of covetousness, the need for prestige, power and blind determination, which manifested itself in one person. Someone so consumed to have what he wanted, and felt it was owed to him, that he allowed no one or no thing obstruct his goal. Destruction and chaos lay in the lives of those whose paths happened to cross his.

Detective Richardson was someone who could put the pieces of the puzzle together. He was the one man who could stop the tempest. The question was could he figure it out in time. Could he prevent evil from devouring good, or was he in fact the catalyst which began a chain of events which could destroy the world of two people who finally found all they had been looking for, all they had ever hoped for or dreamed of in a life's partner.

Poem

We can sit along the roadside and watch life pass us by.

We can reject what is and live in divergent minds by

creating alternate worlds in which to live out our hopes and

dreams.

OR

We can live our lives with the cards that are dealt us,

whether by our own hand or by that which we have no

control.

We can do what is right, for right is always better than the

self-served.

We can embrace our time with acceptance and gratitude,

Taking risks to allow someone close.

OR

We can want for what has never been and miss it when it

comes our way.

The Meeting

It was just another day like any other day. Already an hour into the workday, the morning chatter in the office had quieted down some. Yet, with the desks being so close together it was still difficult to block out the noise to concentrate on the day's work. Laura opened up the bottom left hand drawer of her desk and pulled out her radio headset. She lifted her black oversized sweater to attach the pocket radio to her pant belt and slipped the headset on with the left portion of the earphones resting on her ear and the right side behind her ear. This was so she could hear the phone if necessary. She wove the headset cord under her sweater and attached it to the radio as she switched it on. News, weather, and traffic came across the airwaves. "Good," she thought to herself. "I didn't miss Rush's opening monologue." A faint smile crossed her face.

The phone rang, and she quickly pulled the headphones off. "Used car DMV, this is Laura, can I help you? Yes sir, when did you buy your car?" she said as she reached for her logbook and opened it to

October. "Your name sir, that's Curtis with a 'C' correct? I show your DMV paperwork was sent in to clear on November fifth... No sir that is not an extraordinarily long time. DMV requires we post on sold cars within thirty days and submit to clear within fifty days. Your DMV paperwork was submitted at the forty-day mark to clear. Therefore, it was actually sent in early." Silence hung in the air for about thirty seconds before Laura replied, "No, I am **not** just slow. I just happened to know the person who bought this car was a royal pain in the ass. So, I decided to wait 'til the last possible moment to do **your** paperwork, just to piss you off!" Laura slammed down the phone on the receiver. "God, I hate this desk," Laura grumbled as she looked up to see several women in the office staring at her.

Ginny, who had been seated across from Laura since the day she started working at the dealership, looked at Laura in amazement.

"You didn't do what I think you just did, did you?"

Rolling her eyes Laura responded, "No, He hung up a while ago. I just couldn't resist saying what I really wanted to tell that Adam Henry."

Ginny sighed and returned to her seat to continue with her work.

"Thank God." She muttered.

Laura had put the headset back on only to be interrupted again by Jennifer. Jennifer placed her hands on her desk and leaned forward with a smirk on her face said, "I know what you need, you need a night on the town, a night away from your boys, work, and that dungeon you call home or should I say that home that is your dungeon."

"Ah Jennifer, not this again," Laura sighed, thinking she did not know if she could handle this conversation yet again.

"Yes, this again, you never do anything. You work, go home, sleep and come back to work. There's more to life than work and your boys. Anyway, you did your job. Your boys are all grown up now. You can allow some time to yourself to go out and live a little. Have a little fun. It's not a sin to have fun you know."

Laura's frustration with Jen's persistence to drag her to the clubs had finally tipped the scales on her usually calm demeanor. She snapped back at Jen with raw emotion. "No, it is not a sin to have fun. I just don't consider going to clubs, drinking, and getting picked up by strange men, fun."

"How would you know, you've never tried it." Jennifer snapped back.

"Well I have lived that life vicariously through you, and from what I've heard, I think I'll pass." Laura's sarcasm poured out.

"Hey, what's that suppose to mean?" Jennifer was genuinely surprised.

Laura did not hold back with the disgust she felt about Jennifer's life style. "Ah, come on Jen, since your divorce you've been on the prowl, looking for a man. With the stories you tell, I think any man will do, just so you won't have to be alone. It's no way for a woman your age to act."

Jennifer responded with a wounded voice. "That was cruel. At least I have a life. You know sometimes you can be so condescending."

Laura took a deep breath, looked down somewhat, exhaled, then looked up to apologize to Jennifer, but she had already gone back to her desk. She was thumbing through papers on her desk with diligence, refusing to look up. Laura sat back in her chair then looked up to see

Ginny shaking her head giving her an expression of, 'Well! You did it again!'

Without delay, the headphones went back on Laura's head and she realized she had missed Rush's opening dialog. 'Damn,' she cursed then proceeded with the mountain of papers strewn on her desk.

About an hour later the horn of the lunch truck blew. Laura, upon hearing it, left her desk and walked over to Jennifer.

"Jen, I apologize. Sometimes, I just don't know when to keep my opinions and observations to myself." Laura was sincere in her apology.

Jennifer did not acknowledge that Laura had even spoken. Fretting that she had irreparably offended Jennifer, she made another attempt to make amends. "Come on Jen, it's not like we haven't discussed all of this stuff. You never took it this hard before." Laura turned to look at the vendor outside and then back to Jennifer. "Hey, I'll treat you to a muffin off the roach coach as a peace offering. How 'bout it?"

Jennifer's eyes met Laura's. A broad smiled crossed her face and with a devious tone in her voice, she announced her choice of a peace offering.

"Nah, let's have a real lunch and go to Maria's."

"Jen, I brought my lunch." Laura countered.

"Come on it's our favorite Mexican restaurant. Anyway, you always bring your lunch; then you don't really take a lunch. You just quickly eat and then work through lunch. When was the last time you went out for lunch? I don't mean running to the nearest fast food restaurant grabbing a burger or something equally disgusting, but actually going out, taking the full hour you're entitled to and having a real meal?" Jennifer pleaded.

"You know I can't afford to do that." Laura said exasperated.

"Fine then I'll treat and maybe we well be back in an hour and maybe we won't." Jennifer said quite matter of fact.

"Jen, I've got a lot of work to do. I can't afford to...does this mean I'm forgiven?" Laura said, finally figuring out Jennifer's tactic.

At this point Jennifer displayed an open fondness for Laura.

"You know I can't stay mad at you. You're my best friend. You're the only one who cares enough to tell it like it is and tries to keep me walking the straight and narrow. Not that I listen. Well, I listen, I just don't do it." Jennifer took a deep breath then continued, "John called last night. He announced he and his twenty year old slut are pregnant and getting married."

Now Laura understood why Jennifer was so anxious to leave the office. Her tone of voice dramatically changed, and was full of compassion. "I'm sorry Jen." She whispered.

Jennifer snatched up her purse, from under her desk, to check her wallet. As she thumbed through, counting the money inside, she spoke without looking up.

"Well, he's finally getting that child I could never give him. Damn, not only was I dumped for a girl young enough to be his daughter, but one with a firm ass, thighs, and tits. She gets the man and the life I had always hoped for. I hope she puts on a hundred pounds with this pregnancy." Jennifer spewed, looking almost as though she was talking to her purse.

Laura began to feel uneasy about this conversation taking place in the office. Her eyes met with Jennifer's. Jennifer, desperate to hide her pain, made a weak attempt to smile. Laura could not resist her friend and acquiesced to her request. "Come on, Maria's is beckoning."

Jennifer flung her purse over her shoulder and took hold of Laura's arm. In her usual flippant manner she temporarily brushed off the days woes.

"You know it girl. It's not as good as sex or mocha java ice-cream, but close."

Laura shook her head dumbfounded at how quickly Jennifer could recuperate. "That's my Jen."

The scratchy sounds of Mexican music could be heard through the ceiling speakers. The lighting was very low compared to the outdoors, and it was difficult to read the menus before them. The busboy had left water, chips, and salsa between them. Jennifer took a chip and dipped it in the salsa, and as she did she stared across the table. "What are you going to have?"

Laura responded without looking up. "The usual, chile rellenos."

Jennifer placed her menu down and stared at Laura in amazement.

"Geeeesssh, you are stuck in your ways! Why do you bother to even look at the menu?"

Laura peeked over the top of the menu to see Jennifer's eyes glaring back. "What? I like them and I rarely get to eat out. So yes, I order the same thing most every time. What's wrong with that?"

The mischievous side of Jennifer snuck in. She decided to change the subject on her friend. "Laura, take a chance do something different, go the Black Stallion with me on Friday."

Laura emitted a deep sigh, "If nothing else, you are persistent. No, I think it's more than that. Tenacious would be more accurate. Here I thought you were going to suggest something like, 'Laura, try the Calamari, you'll love it."

The waitress interrupted the conversation to take their order. Laura ordered her Chile Rellenos with ice tea, and Jennifer ordered the taco salad and a diet cola remarking how she had to watch her figure. The waitress took the order, pan faced, and left.

Jennifer figured she would press the issue since Laura had not snapped back with the usual 'no' to a night out. "So, that means you'll go Friday?"

"No, that doesn't mean I'll go Friday." Laura laughed.

Jennifer quipped back without hesitation. "Fine then, Saturday it is. That way it will give you all day to decide what to wear and get ready for your big, if not your only night *ever* out on the town."

Before Laura could respond, the waitress had placed their respective drinks in front of them. Laura took two sugar packets and poured them into the glass. She fidgeted with the straw while trying to figure a way out of this line of questioning. Jennifer impatient for an answer, pressed on.

"Well? Are you going Saturday, or what?"

Laura knew she had to say something to release her grip on the subject, so she came up with the only thing that popped into her mind.

"Jen, you know I don't even know how to dance to that country western music."

Jennifer leaned forward and spoke in almost a whisper. "I bet you've had sex since the last time you went dancing, and we both know how long it's been since you've had sex. Are you a virgin again?"

Laura placed her chin on her fist looking like the statue of the thinker.

"You'd think so."

"Don't you get lonely? I mean don't you ever miss having a man in your bed?" Jennifer asked, more to affirm her own actions to combat the loneliness than to discern Laura's feelings.

"Yeah, I get lonely. Sometimes, I get stark raving mad lonely. At times, I feel as though I am starving to death emotionally for adult companionship. However, there are advantages to sleeping alone. No one steals my covers, there's no drool on my pillow cases, I don't have to try to roll the man over so he will stop snoring in my ear, **and** I'd have more than four inches of bed in which to sleep on."

"Granted, but cuddling up to a warm body instead of a cold pillow appeals to me." Jennifer popped back.

"Jen, you are still a beautiful woman regardless of what that Adam Henry of an ex-husband told you. You don't have to act so desperate. You've got time. You don't have to settle. I'll never understand why you think you have to eat a pound of manure to have a broken Oreo cookie. Anyway, at our age the hot flashes are coming and you'll be pushing that warm body away saying I'm too hot, I'm too hot." Laura tried to bolster Jennifer's self image.

They never could have a complete conversation that stayed serious and Jennifer was one who could not let anyone have the last word. "One, I could never be too hot and two, are you trying to ruin my appetite just in time for the food?" she said fanning herself with the menu.

The waitress placed their meals before them. Laura lowered her head for just a moment then began eating. Jennifer again stared at her friend, somewhat envious of her beliefs and convictions. Yet, she was determined to cling to wild ways. For Jennifer, it was a matter of survival.

"Hm, there you go again trying to keep me on the straight and narrow, always trying to correct my ways. I think you should give up this quest of yours; I'm hopeless you know," Jennifer said as she stabbed her salad.

Laura cut off a piece of her chile rellenos. As she brought the fork to her mouth, she hesitated to address Jennifer's last remark. "My saying a little prayer before my meal is not an attempt on my part to keep you on the 'straight and narrow' as you put it. But since you brought it up I will give up this quest to drag you to church if you give up your quest to get me to go out and live life as you call it?"

Jennifer just about spit her taco salad out, "Hell no!"

Laura took another bite mulling over Jennifer's persistence. It appeared today she was walking on eggshells. So, she needed to display a demeanor of calm when she spoke. "Well, I guess we have a stalemate then. Anyway, you know I'm right. You know the only person you're hurting is yourself, and you'll never find what you're looking for at clubs."

"Well, at least I'm looking. Did you ever look? I mean did you ever try dating."

Jennifer waited, hoping that Laura would for once open up and let her into her life, at least a little. Laura sat in silence for a moment trying to think how she could word what she is about to say, divulging enough to satisfy Jen's curiosity, but not say more than she was comfortable talking about.

"About a year after Bob died I thought maybe I should. The boys were young then and they needed a father, a man in their life. Someone who could counter balance the mommy factor. You know someone who could bring them through their rite of passage."

"You've been reading again, haven't you?" Jennifer interjected.

Laura leaned forward and touched Jennifer's hand.

"Hello, I'm finally telling you my life story here and you're interrupting. Do you want to hear this or what?"

Jennifer held her hands up in a motion of surrender.

"I'll be quiet, promise."

"So anyway, I found I didn't attract the kind of man I wanted. I seemed to choose badly, sometimes, very badly. Most of the men I met were divorced with very angry ex-wives that they had to contend with because of the children. Then the children; I thought mine were difficult, but these kids were totally unruly. Weekend Dad's who spoil the kids rotten because of guilt and who are constantly being dragged back to court for one thing, or another, usually more money, was more than I had bargained for, or wanted.

Then there were the ones who had never been married and I don't think ever intended to get married much less take on the responsibility of two young boys. So, I said the hell with it and moved into my parent's house. They made the upstairs into an apartment for us so we could have our privacy, and I let my dad be dad to my kids."

Jennifer waited for Laura to continue, but she did not.

"So where's all the juicy dating details I kept quiet for? Hmmm?"

Laura sat back in her chair and stated as matter a fact, "There's none. My life has been pretty boring, difficult, but boring."

Jennifer was still trying to put the pieces together and continued to question her. "So how come you moved out of your folk's house?"

Laura did not like talking about the tragedies in her life. She had always kept people at what she considered a safe distance, but as of late she had felt a need to bring people in a little closer. Jennifer and she had a friendship that mirrored the odd couple, but all and all she trusted her. She was the kind of friend that would give you the shirt off her back if you needed it, so she took a breath and started to share this aspect of her story in the only way she knew how, short n' sweet.

"Mom got real sick, cancer. It was a long and agonizing death. After Mom died, Dad sold the house to pay all the medical bills. We bought the mobile home, and he stayed there with us until he died last year."

Her father's death was a memory she could not bare to talk about. His loss bit deep into her heart. A wound she was not yet ready to share with anyone, not even Jennifer. She took the last bite of her meal and decided it was time to leave. "Come on, it's time to get back."

Jennifer knew at this point the conversation was over. There was no sense trying to push the issue any further.

As they walked outside to the parking lot, the sunlight just about blinded them. It took a few moments for their eyes to adjust. As Laura unlocked the car door, Jennifer rested her head on her forearms on top of the hood of the car. For a moment, she was pensive. Then, feeling the need to respond to Laura's disapproval of her life style, she too allowed herself a moment of vulnerability. "Laura, I do know your right. It's just after twenty years of marriage, sleeping with the man I loved and thought I'd grow old with; I found I just can't bear to be alone. Perhaps, once I'm over the initial shock I'll settle down and fly right."

Laura continued to be amazed how Jennifer could justify and qualify her behavior. She used her sarcasm to bring a point home. "Jen, it's been two years now. I think the shock has worn off, and you're just in a very bad habit or should I say just behaving very badly. I worry about you. Do you have yourself checked for STD's?"

Surprised by the question, Jennifer stuttered, "STD's, what kind of trash do you think I'm sleeping with?"

Laura pursed her lips making a disapproving facial gesture. "The man kind. You know the kind of man that will go to bed with a woman after dancing with her at some club. He has had a few drinks, a little conversation, therefore he knows her. She looks pretty enough through his alcohol blurred eyes. Thus, in his mind it's only the next course of action. Don't tell me you never went to bed with someone the same night you met him, cuz if you do I'll have to tell all the girls at the office you've been lying to us for two years."

"Shit… yes I've been to the doctors. FYI, I don't do that anymore. I had a scare a couple of months back. Fortunately, it was treatable, but next time it may not be. I got my wake up call, but that doesn't mean I'm going to hibernate."

Laura could not resist needling her.

"See, there is hope for you yet."

***

At a new housing tract development in northern Moreno Valley, the sound of saws, hammers, and bulldozers had stopped. Several pickup trucks leaving the site kicked up dust as Josh sat with his legs dangling over the unfinished floor on the second story of the house he had been working on. A sandwich in his left hand he waved his right hand in front of him as though shoeing flies away. "Damn those guys. No matter how many times I tell them not to speed out of here, they do it any ways. They listen as well as my kid did. Num, num…Dust and salami sandwich. Hey Dave, you gonna join me?"

Dave and Josh had worked together for years. In fact, Josh had sponsored Dave's apprenticeship into the electrician's union. Dave responded from the back of the house. "In a minute, I'm looking for the razors, and the wire strippers, and the hammer and the…." Dave's voice trailed off and then he appeared a little behind Josh and to his right, carrying a toolbox in his right hand, a brown paper bag and a thermos in his left. "Where the hell are all the tools? The only things left in here are a Phillips head, a couple of drill bits, and some electrical tape." Dave quizzed.

Josh with his mouth full of sandwich mumbled, "I fink they're on the furst flawr." He swallowed, "In the kitchen." Josh looked at the not quite empty toolbox and then at Dave's sandwich that he had pulled out of a brown paper bag. He sneered with disgust. "Peanut butter and bologna?"

"No," Dave corrects, "Peanut butter, bologna and mayonnaise."

Dave sat down next to Josh, as Josh spat like he was getting something distasteful out of his mouth. "That's worse yet. Which one made that for you, Trisha, or Alicen?"

Dave looked halfhearted at his lunch and pulled the pieces of bread apart to examine its contents. "Trisha, it amazes me that she wouldn't be caught dead bringing a lunch to school, but she always makes sure good ol' dad has a lunch. I know I complain now, but in another year she will be off to college, and I'll be left to make my own lunch, or tag along with the snot nose kids to some fast food joint." Dave waved off in the direction of the now settled cloud of dust.

Josh looked over in the direction of where the pickup trucks had kicked up the dirt, and then with a very serious look on his face, turned to his partner.

"I don't think they leave to actually eat lunch, Dave. I heard they've been seen leaving some topless joint in town. It's not exactly the type of place to fill your belly." Josh patted himself on his well-fed abdomen and continued, "Eye full maybe, belly full, highly unlikely. Besides, you know Joyce will be more than happy to pack a lunch for you. In fact, she would be hurt if you didn't let her."

Dave smiled one of those half smiles. Throughout the years, Josh and Joyce had been surrogate grandparents for his daughters. He was closer to them than their own son. "Yep, the great philosopher. You know you've got a good woman there, Josh. Damn, she's close to being a saint for putting up with you all these years," he said as he gave Josh a light punch to his upper arm.

Josh had already started his desert, homemade apple pie, as Dave took his first bite of his lunch. He thought for a moment as he devoured Joyce's labor of love. "Yeah, you're right on both counts. Hey, Justin bought a new computer and brought over his old one so we could come into the New Year in style. Damn, outside of turning it on and playing card games, of which I always manage to lose at, I have no use for it. Do you think Trisha would like it? You're more than welcome to come by tonight and take it. Please take it. I'm tired of loosing at poker to that blasted machine."

"Yeah, that would be great. The girls have been after me for years to get a computer. Supposedly, so they can write their papers for school, but I've been putting it off after hearing all the horror stories of these on-line junkies and the chat room nightmares. I've had more than my fair share of people with addictions in my life. Lord knows I don't need anymore. Does it have a printer?" Dave asked.

"Yeah, but I could never get it to work right. It just spits out gobbly goop. As far as that on-line stuff, just don't buy the service and you don't have to worry about it. I'm sure Trisha can live without it. Heck, she lived without a computer for seventeen years; she'll survive. So, what are you doing this weekend? Now that soccer's over, it should be pretty quiet on the home front these days, yeah?"

Dave set down his half-eaten sandwich and opened his thermos to wash down the almost palatable sandwich. "Nope, it would be. Alicen will be working at the hospital all weekend and Trisha is going on a church retreat, but my brother is going to Vegas to get married again. He wanted to have a bachelor party, but his fiancée slash shack up honey nixed that one. Just as well, I would have had to decline the stripper party. It just drives me nuts to see girls close to my daughter's ages degrading themselves for a bunch of drunks. So, I agreed to go to his favorite haunt for his last night as a single man."

Josh was taken aback. "You're going to a single's bar. Dang, I've got to mark this one down on the calendar. How many is this for the little brother?"

"It's not a single's bar! It's country western dance place." Dave snapped back defensively, and then answered Josh's question. "This is number three. Maybe he'll get it right this time. I doubt it; he doesn't seem to know how to keep it in his pants."

"It's a singles bar just with a twang slant to it. Number three, damn, he doesn't stay married long enough to get through the honeymoon much less learn how to live with them."

"Yeah, I know. Come on, let's get back to work and maybe we can leave this place early today. That way I can stop by and pick up that glorified stack of cards."

"Sounds like a plan Stan. Hey, hand me the keys to your truck I need to get the drill out." Josh requested.

Dave fished into his front right hand pocket and pulled out a set of keys with just three keys on it, house key, truck key, and tool chest key. He threw them to Josh and then trekked down to the kitchen area to locate the missing tools while Josh meandered over to the truck.

In the kitchen, Dave located what appeared to be most of the tools strewn on the floor in various places. He shook his head and thought to himself, 'That Josh looses more tools.' He picked up the tools and placed all but the wire strippers back into the tool box then left the box on the floor where Josh was working.

Josh had pulled himself up on the side step of the truck and took the key marked with a skull and cross bone. He proceeded to place the key in the lock only to notice the lid was a tad ajar. Josh pondered, 'It's not like Dave **not** to lock this thing up. Hmm, what's up with that?' Having lifted the lid open, he looked inside, but did not see the power drill. He scratched his head and thought, 'I know he always keeps it here on the left side of the chest. He must have forgotten it.' Josh returned the lid to close the tool chest, locked it then huffed and puffed his way back to the house. Somewhat out of breath, he yelled out, "Hey Dave, did you forget to put the drill in this morning? Do you have a girlfriend I don't know about?"

Dave peered down the unfinished stairwell where Josh was standing.

"Josh, what the Hell are you talking about? I put the drill in last night after I finished putting up some bookshelves for Alicen and what's this about a girlfriend?"

"Well, I figured the only thing that would distract you from the meticulous care you take of the tools would be a love interest."

"Believe me Josh you would be the first to know if I had a love interest. Are you sure you didn't take the drill out this morning? You know how you misplace things."

Josh looked up deep in thought, closed his eyes then opened them. "Yep, I'm sure, plus the tool chest was unlocked. I *know* better than to leave that unlocked. There would be hell to be pay for a month of Sundays. Something's not right here."

"Your right. I'm going to go down to tell Nick that we probably have a thief on the premises. Damn, I've only had that drill for a couple of months."

Dave and Josh walked to the front of the house. As they did, the parade of pickup trucks sped back onto the site. While they watched them park, a very old beat up white pickup truck straggled in. Two men, in their mid to late twenty's, exited the truck while it four cycled, backfired, and then shut down. Dave glared at the two men. "They give me the creeps. I don't trust those guys. They always keep to themselves. I think Nick scraped the bottom of the barrel when he hired those two. I don't know what he was thinking about. I'll be back in a little while."

Dave rambled toward the mobile office. As he entered the building, he could hear Nick's booming voice talking on the phone. Nick was the current General Manager for the construction site. He had a formidable if not down right intimidating presence about him. When Nick stood, his stature diminished Dave's six-foot, two hundred pound frame. Not many challenged his authority or demands and were around the next day to tell of it. He had a memory for detail that was near photographic, and when he was given a job deadline, he seldom missed it. Nick held up his hand with one finger up as to say, 'Just a minute.' He continued to speak to the person on the phone without looking up.

"I want to know when you are going to make the delivery. The shipment was supposed to be here this afternoon." There was silence with the occasional sounds of acknowledgment. Then Nick's demeanor became very animated.

"An additional fee, I don't think so. If you have to do a rush delivery, that is not my problem. The contract specifies supplies of a certain quantity for a specified price to be delivered in segments on certain dates. If you can't hold up your end of the contract, I can void the whole damn thing... No, I am not going to pay my guys time and a half to come in here to unload and secure the shipment on a Saturday… No, that's not my problem lady, read your contract. It says normal working hours, that's Monday through Friday eight to five. Have I made myself perfectly clear? … If Monday is the soonest you can get it here fine, but no later." Nick slammed down the phone then turned to his bookkeeper. "Grace, can you call these incompetent idiots first thing Monday morning and make sure our shipment is on its way?"

Grace looked up from her computer screen in her usual calm manner.

"No problem."

Then Nick turned his attention to Dave who was looking at the site map and the time schedules. "Dave, what can I do for you?"

Dave explained the situation with the missing drill. Nick appeared to be very concerned. "Unfortunately, you're not the first to report missing power tools. Last week Al reported a Skil saw missing. Grace, have Dave fill out a report and tell security to be sure they lock this place down real tight this weekend. Okay?" Grace nodded in agreement and Nick returned his attention to Dave. "The insurance should have you paid back in about thirty days. Hopefully, I can get to the bottom of this quickly."

Dave thanked Nick for his time. As he walked back to the house, he checked out the two ne'er-do-well's loading trash into a truck. The skinny red head stopped, lit up a cigarette, and stared back at him. Dave nodded as though to say, 'Howdy,' but he just glared at him then turned back to loading the truck.

After finishing the installation of the bathroom switches and built-in light fixtures, Dave came down stairs to find Josh. He glanced down at his watch.

"Damn, it's almost a quarter to five. Josh let's pack up and get out of here. We were going to leave early. Remember? Now we're going to hit all that blasted traffic."

One thing about Josh, you never had to prod him along to leave for the day. Before Dave uttered his last word, Josh had the toolbox in hand and was already on his way to the truck. Dave unlocked the tool chest, opened the toolbox to check it contents, and then he closed it placing it in its own special place in the chest. Having entered the truck, Dave behind the wheel, Josh stuck a tape labeled 'The Best of Mozart' into the cassette player. They both settled in for the long drive home. As always Josh said, "Home, James."

Dave smiled, "Dave, I keep telling you my name is Dave."

***

Saturday morning, it was Laura's chance to sleep in. The morning light was filtering through the bedroom curtains. Laura could hear the faint sound of the morning rain. She sat up and opened the window a few more inches so she could also smell the fresh damp air mixed with the dry earth. She lay back down, pulling the extra pillow over her eyes to block the light. She snuggled up in her pile of blankets, feeling at peace with the world, until Newt, her gray and black tabby jumped up and demanded her attention. Newt purred as he kneaded on the blankets covering her. Laura obliged his persistence by petting him, and then she picked him up, slid out of bed, and placed him back down. As she put on her sweats, she talked to her cat.

"Okay, okay. You did it. I'm up. Are you happy now? Well, so much, for my sleeping in. Thanks Newt."

Laura walked into the kitchen and turned on the coffee maker. She collected the dirty dishes from the counter and various other places through the house. Then she placed them in the sink and filled it with warm water. In the laundry room, she sorted through the week's laundry placing towels in the washer with soap and turned the knob to the wash cycle. Smelling the coffee, she returned to the kitchen. The pot had filled about two cups worth and she took a mug out of the cabinet and poured her first cup of the day. With her coffee, note pad and pen in hand she exited out the sliding glass door to the patio. Seated at the outside table she sipped her coffee and made her weekend list.

> *Morning walk*
> *Laundry*
> *Clean house*
> *Groc shopping*
> *Turn soil in garden*
> *Weed*
> *Exchange pant outfit*
> *Pull out Christmas decorations*
> *Buy tree/decorate*

'Well," she thought "that should keep me busy enough. Hm… maybe if I get done early I'll have time to work on my painting."

Picking up the coffee and pad, she returned inside for a second cup. As she poured her coffee, her eldest son Matt wandered out, his robe on, but not tied. His flannel boxers and hairy chest glared through the opening of his robe. Laura greeted him in her usual manner.

"Good morning. You're up early."

Matt ran his fingers though his already thinning blonde hair.

"Yeah, I know. They scheduled me from eight to five at work today. Can I have a cup?"

Laura poured him a cup, adding cream and sugar. Matt tied his robe then took the coffee.

"I know this time of year I sure can use the money, but these late nights then morning shifts don't leave much time for sleep much less a social life. I have to shower. Is there anything I can eat before I leave?"

Laura looked over at the sink full of dirty dishes, wishing her boys were more helpful on their own.

"I'll make some french toast. Do you need anything for lunch?"

"No lunch today Mom. Thanks anyway. Just got paid so I'll be eating out for a change. French toast sounds good."

With his coffee in hand, he entered the bathroom, turned on the shower, cd player, and then closed the bathroom door. Laura reflected on how quickly he grew up.

Breakfast placed on the counter, Matt came out of his room with hands full.

"Check list, change of clothes." He presented a hanger with shirt and pants. "Jacket, keys, deodorant, wallet, razor, and cologne. I think that's everything. I'll be home late tonight. Sara and I are going to the movies after work."

Laura directed his attention to his food. While he was devouring his breakfast she proceeded to do her motherly job of ascertaining her son's activities.

"What are you two going to see?"

"Well, if Sara has it her way we will see some tragic love story, and if I have it my way we'll see a shoot 'em up, blood and guts action film. I wonder if there is a double feature with one of each, then we would both be in movie heaven. Eh, I doubt it."

Matt glanced up at the clock. Time had slipped away from him as usual. He stuffed the last of his breakfast into his mouth and washed it down with a gulp of coffee. He collected his clothes, grabbed a plastic grocery bag from a drawer in the kitchen, and placed all his miscellaneous belongings in the bag. He gave his mom a kiss on the cheek and proceeded out the side door. As he started to shut the door, a car pulled up.

"Hey Mom, is Jennifer walking with you this morning?"

"No, why?"

Laura edged herself towards the door where Matt was standing to see who had arrived.

"Well, she's here so you better go hide. OOPS, too late, she saw us." Matt gave her his best smile, "Hi Jennifer. How are you doing this morning?"

Jennifer looked up at him. It was obvious she had been crying.

"Ah oh, it's going to be a long day for you, Mom. I'm outta here." Matt whispered.

"Chicken!" Laura whispered back.

Matt planted behind the wheel of his semi-restored '70 bug, looked over at Jennifer then at his mother, assessing the situation.

"You've got that right!"

Laura waved a tired wave at Matt and shouted, "Have a good time; tell Sara I said Hi!"

As Matt left, Laura muttered, "and drive safely."

Jennifer came up the steps towards Laura with a whimper in her voice. Without so much as a good morning she started in. "John called again last night. It appears the pregnancy was a false alarm, and now his little girl is not sure she wants a baby, or to get married."

"Jen, why do you do this to yourself? Why do you allow that man to torture you with his love problems? You're divorced remember? He left you for the younger woman; you didn't leave him. I bet he told you how much he misses you and how he still loves you."

Jennifer looked up at Laura, misty eyed, and then shook her head in a yes motion, just like a little girl. Laura as always offered her comfort.

"Come on in Jen. I've got coffee and a box of tissues waiting for you inside."

Laura placed her arm around Jennifer, and she collapsed onto Laura's shoulder. An uncontrollable wave of sobs wrenched her body. Laura held her for a moment then guided her to the kitchen counter where Matt had just finished breakfast. She cleared the counter and handed Jennifer a box of tissues then poured her a cup of coffee. She leaned against the kitchen counter while Jennifer wiped her eyes and blew her nose trying to regain her composure.

"I.... I know I shouldn't let him dump on me like that, but I never could say no to the man."

"Come on girl, stiff upper lip. You can be strong. You can let him go and you *can* find contentment in your life."

Laura felt compassion and maybe a little pity for Jennifer and she always tried to bring up something positive no matter how dire the situation. Then Laura decided she needed to change her tone with Jennifer and spoke with her mother voice.

"But you have to first stop taking John's calls. I don't care if it means you put call blocking on your phone, change your phone number, or move to another country, you just have to put a stop to it. Do you understand what I am saying and why I'm saying it?"

Jen looked up with her big brown puppy dog eyes, sad as they could be, nodding her head in acknowledgment. "Cuz, I'm only hurting myself, right?"

"Right, also when you stay this attached, this invested in him you won't really allow anyone else to get close and you'll miss that ship when it comes in."

Jennifer having somewhat regained her composure queried, "Are you trying to tell me if I don't let go I'll end up a lonely old maid like you?"

"Yeah, something like that." Laura said somewhat astounded at her jibe.

"I guess I'll just have to help you remedy that."

"Ah oh, here she goes. You recuperate awfully fast girl."

"Yep, and it's Saturday and you know what that means?"

"I suppose your going to play on my sympathies too?"

"If it works, you bet. I don't want to stay home alone tonight and I certainly don't want to hang around here. Talk about depressing."

Laura was proud of her little home and took a little offense to Jennifer's remark. "What's so depressing about being here?"

"No live music, no dancing, no good looking men to gawk at…"

Just then, Laura's youngest straggled out of his room and headed for the bathroom and Jennifer backtracked her last remark.

"No offense Kyle."

Kyle shrugged his shoulders as he closed the bathroom door.

"None taken."

Jennifer's eyes never left Kyle as he passed by. His appearance had drastically changed since the last time she saw him. Almost in shock, Jennifer asked in a whisper, "Did he shave his eyebrows off?"

Laura had a difficult time containing her frustration and disgust with her son's counter culture behavior. "From what I can tell he has shaved all bodily hair off, except for the head obviously."

"Kids! I'd give anything not to have to shave and that hair I've spent more money trying to be blond! He is and he dyes his hair black."

"You missed the tattoos."

"No way! They're hidden by his clothes, right?"

"I wish."

"How does he expect to get a job with tattoos showing?"

Laura rubbed her face with both her hands in total exasperation.

"Don't know, and I don't think he cares. He has changed so much since my Dad died, plus he found out girls like the rebel. The tattoos started when he turned eighteen, and he knew I couldn't stop him, but what he doesn't seem to understand, I don't **have** to let him live here anymore. He wants to be an adult and live his life his way. He can also take on the responsibilities that go along with it."

"You wouldn't throw him out on the street, would you?"

A deep sadness crept into Laura's voice. "Believe me I'm toying with it. Maybe drop him off at some shelter." Laura paused as she watched Kyle return to his room. Her eyes welled up, and the sadness overwhelmed her. "It breaks my heart to see him so lost, so without direction in his life. Yet in the same breath I feel he is taking advantage of my love for him. He believes I won't ever really put my foot down and stand my ground. I'm not sure he's wrong, but how do you motivate someone who has no motivation?"

"I don't envy you, and I've wondered that same question when it comes to you."

"What are you talking about?"

"Going out, dating. You probably should meet someone first then date them."

"Oh, how could I forget, your quest."

"That's right. My quest."

Laura thought for a moment then made her proposal. "Okay, here's the deal. I'll go with you tonight if you promise on your life and our friendship you'll go to church with me tomorrow. Deal?"

Jennifer responded without a second thought. "Deal! It's not going to help."

Laura responded in kind, "Well, I don't think going out to a club is going to help either. So we are at check mate, again!"

Jennifer had a puzzled look on her face as she pondered the words 'check mate.' "Dang, I don't even know how to play chess."

"For someone who doesn't know how to play, you play the game quite well." Laura grinned

---

Jennifer picked up her purse, grabbed a few more tissues as she prepared to leave.

"I'll be by at nine to pick you up. Wear something real pretty. I know you have something in that closet of yours."

Laura walked with her over to the door. "I'll drive my own car and follow you, just in case... I haven't a clue as to what I'll wear."

As Jennifer walked down the back steps, she turned to her friend.

"Drive your own car if you must, but promise me you'll dress up and touch up your hair, the gray is showing through."

"It will be dark in there no one will notice."

Jennifer groped into the abyss of her purse to find her car keys. She stopped in mid stride then stepped back up to where Laura was standing giving her a big hug.

"Thank you." She mouthed.

Laura stood at the door, and watched Jennifer pull out of the driveway. Leaning against the door jam she sighed, "What did I just get myself into?"

Having taken care of what she could on her to do list, Laura decided to check her closet for that 'something pretty.' For every item she pulled out, she had a comment. "Too small, too old, too revealing, not comfortable, and oh god, I'd have to wear panty hose." This was not going well.

Seated on her bed, she pet Newt who had been cat napping. She spoke as though she was talking to the cat, but she was really just thinking out loud to herself. "I never thought I'd be one of those women who would stand in front of a closet full of clothes and say, 'I have nothing to wear.' What to do, Newt? What to do? It's too late to go out and get something."

Newt opened his eyes for a moment, then acting bored with the whole ordeal went back to sleep. Laura sat there staring at her closet full of clothes, wishing she had never made this deal with Jennifer. Out of the corner of her eye, she noticed a bag sitting on the top shelf.

"Oh yeah, huh. I have that pant outfit I was going to return. The one I bought to go to the Christmas party and decided not to go to cuz I would have been odd man (woman) out. You know the black one with the embroidered red poinsettias on the top. Yep, that'll do." Again, she spoke to the disinterested cat. It always seemed a little less crazy if you were talking to the cat and not to yourself. Someone once told her that only crazy people talked to themselves. She had to laugh at herself. "Was it any less crazy to talk to your cat?"

Laura pulled the bag down from the shelf of her closet and then took her change of clothes with her to the bathroom. While showering, she prayed for her boys, for Jennifer, and then for herself.

"Please God let me make it through the night without being a total nervous wreck."

Dried off, with her new clothes on, Laura looked at her reflection in the mirror. Her damp limp hair lay lifeless against her face. The reflection staring back at her revealed the tale-tell signs of ageing. She thought, "No amount of makeup, or hair dye is going to fix this. God, I hate the whole singles scene. Well, I can only do what I can do." She dried her shoulder length dark blonde hair, curled the ends, added a little of Matt's hair gel and brushed it back away from her face. Having applied a minimal amount of makeup, she turned to see how the new clothes looked.

"Another ten or fifteen pounds wouldn't hurt. Ah, shoot, that reminds me, I missed my morning walk."

Kyle knocked on the door. "Mom, you almost done in there?"

Laura opened the door so Kyle could have the bathroom. He just stood there staring at her. Laura was a little unnerved by his glare.

"What? What are you staring at?"

"You, where are you going all dressed up?"

Laura stood up trying to look poised, dignified, and she hoped not too bad too look at. "What do you think?"

Kyle pursed his lips appearing to look as though he was thinking very hard. "Not bad, but you still didn't say where your going."

"Thanks, I think. The answer to the $64 question is, Jennifer and I made a deal, I said I'd go to some club with her, and she said she'd go to church with me."

"If you ask me, Jennifer got the raw end of that deal."

"Well, I didn't ask you."

A car pulled up to the front of the mobile home, the horn honked, the door slammed, and then high heels clicked up the stairs, followed by rapid knocking on the front door. "Come on Laura, open the door it's cold out here."

Laura opened the door and Jennifer rushed in with her arms wrapped around herself. "If it gets any colder I swear it will snow. When are you going to fix the lights out there?" Jennifer asked as she glided through the door.

Judging by Jennifer's outfit it would only need to drop to seventy degrees before she would have caught pneumonia.

"Can't afford an electrician so I guess it will be in God's time, not mine." Laura clarified. "Ah Jen, that's a little skimpy, a little short for a woman your age. Don't you think?" She noted.

"Heck no, there are women older than me who dress like this."

Kyle walked into the front room and turned on the television. "Cool duds, Jennifer."

She smiled and then turned to Laura, "See... My, my, my don't you look pretty! I knew you'd find something, only shoes would help."

Laura glanced down at her bare feet. "I'll be right back."

A few moments later, she hurried out with black boots, white socks, and a black coat in hand. Seated in the rocker next to the couch she proceeded to put on her socks and boots and give Kyle his evening instructions.

"Now Kyle, I don't want you staying up all night watching TV, or playing on that computer and no smoking in the house, okay?"

Kyle picked up the remote and started flipping through the channels.

"Don't worry I won't even be here. I'm going to Tim's house."

Laura's eyes glared at him, "And when were you planning on letting me know?"

He shrugged his shoulders, which Laura correctly interpreted as 'don't know and don't care.'

Laura wanted desperately to respond to Kyle's lack of concern, but this attitude of his always threw her for a loop and left her speechless. Jennifer on the other hand was getting impatient and tugged on Laura's arm.

"Come on. Let's go before all the tables are taken."

Laura stood up and put on her coat. She then walked behind the couch to give Kyle a kiss on the top of his head. "Be good."

"Yeah right." He snapped.

As they headed for the door, Laura could hear Jennifer still beaming over Kyle's comment. "Cool duds, Jennifer." She mimicked.

Hesitating for a moment, Laura stood in the doorway looking at the back of Kyle's head then with a heavy heart closed the door. Walking down the stairs towards the cars, Laura corrected Jennifer's interpretation of Kyle's remark. "Jennifer, I hate to burst your bubble, but Kyle was being sarcastic. Have you seen the way his girlfriend dresses? He *really* thinks that's cool, and she looks like death most the time."

Jennifer ignored Laura's last statement. She opened the car door then shouted back over to Laura. "I'll try not to drive too fast so not to lose you. You know where it is, just in case, don't you?"

Imitating a Texas accent, Laura yelled back, "Yes ma'am, I know where it is. Don't you go worryn' your pretty little head over me."

It was almost forty minutes later, due to a traffic accident on the 10 freeway, before they arrived at the Black Stallion. They parked their cars then headed towards the entrance. About twenty feet from the front door, Laura made an abrupt stop. Noting Laura's apprehension, Jennifer slipped her arm through Laura's. "Lighten up it will be fun."

Laura's stomach was tied in knots. "I don't do lighten up."

Jennifer continued to try to abate Laura's angst. "Yes, you do. I've seen you and take off those glasses, you have such pretty eyes, don't hide them."

Laura took her glasses off and placed them in her purse. She placed her arm through Jennifer's then looked up towards the entrance. "Madame, let us enter the dragon's lair. Perhaps, there will be a knight in shining armor, or two prepared to rescue us from our mundane lives. That is if I can find the front door now."

Jennifer squeezed her arm. "That's what I like about you. I never know what you're going to say."

***

They had only been there for a little over an hour. Yet, Dave's brother was already finishing his third drink and ordering his fourth.

"Hey bartender, give me another."

The bartender glanced up from his glass-washing task, acknowledging the request.

Dave was concerned with his little brother's alcohol consumption. He knew this was a touchy subject, but he had to say something.

"Darrell, slow down man. You've hours of freedom left."

Darrell emptied the last of his drink with one gulp. "Yeah and I'm gonna to enjoy every second of it. All right, more women are arriving. No offense bro', but I really didn't come here to look at your ugly mug. Why don't you lighten up and have a real drink, a man's drink? Oh yeah, that's right you're the good boy, clean and sober all these years."

Dave never could stand being around his brother when he was drinking and he was quick to display his displeasure.

"Asshole."

Darrell was unaffected by his jab, "Yeah, so what's your point?"

The bartender came over to where the two were standing.

"What can I get you gentlemen?" He asked.

Darrell responded with a condescending tone.

"You've got long term damage to your short-term memory man? I'll take another gin and tonic tall, and my bro' there will have a diet cola. This time don't skimp on the gin." He turned to his brother, "Dave you goin' to ask any of these pretty ladies to dance, or you just goin' to stand here and look dumb all night?"

Darrell had managed to push Dave's buttons and he snapped back.

"Well Darrell I thought I'd just stand here and look dumb all night and watch you make a fool of yourself. Besides at the rate you're going, I figure it will be about an hour before I'm scraping your sorry butt off the floor either too drunk to walk, or from losing a fight you'll start."

"I can take care of myself. I've done all right so far without your help, Mr. Guardian Angel."

"That's a matter of opinion."

Darrell slammed his fresh drink down on the bar. "Why the hell did I *even* think I could have a good time with you? I keep thinking things will change with us, but they never do." Darrell downed what was left of his spilt drink in a single gulp then started to walk away. Dave grabbed his arm, and Darrell snapped it away turning towards him. Dave raised both his hands in front of him with his palms open.

"Hey, I'm not here to fight with you. I'll try to lighten up and have a good time, okay? Anyway, they've got a good band here so I just *might* ask someone to dance," Dave said trying to make some sort of amends with his brother.

"Yeah, I'll believe that one when I see it."

"Taking bets?"

Darrell pulled out his wallet, took out two ten-dollar bills, and placed them on the bar. "Got you covered! Now put your money where your mouth is."

Dave matched his twenty while Darrell looked over the sea of people.

"Now, which one are you going to ask?" Darrell asked.

Dave scoped out the dance floor then the surrounding tables. What he found were women with dates, women too young to consider, and women dressed in clothing they would reprimand their daughters for wearing. Tight jeans, short skirts and low cut tops were the clothing of a mantrap woman, not the kind he would take a serious look at. They were good for a one-night stand and that was about it, but he had given up that life style years ago.

"I don't see her yet Darrell, but I'll keep looking."

Darrell grinned and picked up the money from the bar, placing it in his shirt pocket.

"I'll just keep it here for safe keeping, since it's going to be mine anyway."

Dave shook his head as he leaned on the bar. "Don't be so cock sure little brother, don't be so cock sure."

Across the dance hall, he could see two women taking a seat at a table next to the dance floor. Darrell also peered over the crowd to see who Dave was looking at. "Yeah, the one in the short black skirt, the blonde, she's not bad to look at. Good choice."

Dave shook his head again, "No, no, no, Darrell, not that one, the other one."

Darrell puffed air out of one side of his mouth, "That figures, you have the choice of any little sex kitten in here, and you choose the one that will probably turn you down."

"So, the bet's still on? Right?"

Darrell patted his pocket where he had placed the money. "Sure, it's your money, but even if you get a dance, that's all you'll get."

"Is that all you think of?"

"Damn straight, and that's where I'm going right now to go procure some tasty little morsel. Like that pretty little thing."

Darrell walked over to a woman wearing very tight black jeans, black boots, and a red sweater, which was cut so low Dave thought her well endowed bosom would fall out of it if she bent over. They entered the dance floor finding a place and started dancing a two-step. Darrell was a good dancer and Dave did enjoy watching him. Once the women had seen him out on the dance floor, he never had a lack of dance partners for the evening.

The band finished their song and announced a line dance song. Those who could ran out to the floor, and those who could not scurried off before they were trapped. Dave turned to take a drink of his cola and noticed the two ne'er-do-well's from work standing at the next bar. He thought to himself, "I suppose I should be polite." With soda in hand, he walked over to where they were standing.

"Sean, Ramón, how are you doing tonight? It's a good band don't you think?"

Sean picked up his shot glass and swigged it down, slamming the empty glass on the bar. "Hit me again." With his back to Dave, he waited for the bartender to fill his shot glass again. He removed a cigarette out of his pocket and played with it, twirling it between his fingers then placed it in his mouth chewing on the filter.

Ramón had been leaning on the bar with a beer in his hand, looking jittery at Dave. "No man, the band stinks. I hate this shit-kicking music."

Surprised at his response Dave asked, "Why do you come here then?"

"Cuz red here likes it, and the women are easy. So Mr. Nosy now you know, and now you can go away so I can get me some."

Dave realized he had just stepped in where he was not wanted so he backed up. "Just trying to be friendly."

Sean turned around staring at Dave with cold angry eyes, as though he was looking at the most disgusting thing ever created. "Well, you've done your civic duty. You slummed, now you can go."

Sean took his lighter out of his pocket and feigned as though he was going to light the cigarette dangling from his mouth.

Dave hesitantly interjected, "I don't think they allow smoking in here Sean."

"Yeah I know shit-head. You're probably one of the assholes who made sure of that, always looking to take away people's rights, so you goody two shoes don't have to put up with the nasty smell. You always think you're better than everyone else."

Feeling like he had somehow stirred up an angry hornets nest, Dave decided it was time to go. "You guys have a good time." He walked away wondering what he had done to deserve that little mess.

Sean spit on the floor; his eyes never left Dave's back as he walked to his place at the other bar. Ramón hit Sean on the forearm in excitement as a young woman crossed in front of him.

"Whoa! Look at that piece of ass. Oh man, she's just asking for someone to do her."

Sean pushed Ramón away. "I told you never to touch me. Understand asshole?"

His anger threw Ramón for a loop. He had no idea where Sean was coming from. "Damn it, what's your problem?" Ramón spit back.

Sean leaned in towards Ramón with his face just inches from his. "You asshole, you're my problem. If you blow this deal because you can't keep your hands off of things, or keep your mouth shut, your ass is mine. Do you understand?"

"What the hell are you talking about, man? I just want to go get some pussy."

Sean's patience with Ramón was next to none and he never hesitated to indicate so. "I'm not talking about the women, stupid! I'm talking about lifting tools off the site and talking to your buddies' downtown."

"Women like you to show them a good time. They expect it. How the hell do you expect me to live on what they pay us at that lousy job?"

Sean grabbed him by the front of his shirt. His face was bright red and when he spoke, spittle sprayed in Ramón's face. "In a little while asshole, you'll have all the money you want to spend on your whores and then some. But if you blow it, ruin all my planning and the drop doesn't go down… You can kiss your ass good-bye."

Ramón pulled himself away brushing his shirt down and wiping the spittle from his face. Ramón had known Sean for a long time, and he knew once he got angry he stayed angry. You did not mess with him. You did not talk your way out. You just did what he said.

"Hey, I'm cool man. No more lifting tools, and I don't say nothing to the gang. I swear."

Sean glared at Ramón with contempt. "I better not find out different Ramón. I better not find out different."

Sean turned around to the bar, pointed to his shot glass. The bartender obliged. Ramón in the mean time wandered over to a woman in her twenties standing near the dance floor. She had black bouffant hair like some country western singer. He placed his right hand on her buttocks and whispered in her ear. She turned with her drink in her hand and splashed it in his face. "Whore." he said as he walked away wiping his face off for the second time that night. "You'll get yours."

The woman and her friend stared at Ramón's backside as he walked away. One yelled out. "Jerk!"

Ramón turned around. "That's jerk me off, Ladies." He said making an obscene gesture with his hand. Disgusted, the women turned away.

Ramón decided to roam around looking for easier prey. He noticed Dave starting to leave the bar area. Making his way through the mass of bodies, he deliberately bumped into Dave lifting his wallet from his back pocket.

"Sorry man, too much to drink."

Ramón placed the lifted wallet in his jacket pocket and walked away. Dave watched as Ramón staggered away acting as though he was drunk. While Dave's gaze was still locked in on Ramón, Darrell, with sweat running down his forehead, joined Dave from the dance floor. He wiped his forehead with his hand, and then his hand on his jeans.

"Who was that jerk?" He said with labored breath.

Dave refused to take his eyes off Ramón as he walked away.

"Exactly, someone if I never saw again it would be too soon. You having fun?"

"Sure am bubba. We've got good music, good drinks, pretty woman, can't get closer to heaven than this." Darrell pulled the money out of his shirt pocket and handed it to Dave. "Here go buy us another round. I need to go to the head." Darrell headed towards the men's rest room and Dave took the money and placed it in his own shirt pocket. As he did, he noticed the blond leave the table he was checking out earlier. Dave thought to himself, 'Well, no better time than the present.'

The band announced they were taking a break and introduced the DJ. Dave weaved himself through the mass of people, near the table where the women were seated. As Dave moved behind Laura's chair, she pushed her chair out knocking him back, spilling some of his drink down her own blouse.

"Oh god, I'm sorry ma'am. Can I get something to clean that up?"

Laura looked up to see a very attractive man staring back at her. "No, that's okay. It was my fault. It's okay."

Dave reached for the napkin on the table and knocked over her drink. "I'm not making too many points here, am I?"

"I think you owe me one now." Laura said as she smiled.

Dave looked around. Seeing a waitress he summoned her over to the table. "What ever this lady is drinking would you please bring her one, I'm paying."

"What well you have, honey?" The waitress asked Laura.

"Club soda with a squeeze of lime. Please make sure it's a wedge of lime and not just the twist."

"No problem hon, how about you good looking? You look like you could use a fresh one."

"Diet cola and a towel please."

Laura was trying to mop up the spilt drink with an already saturated napkin. "The towel first, please." Laura requested.

Dave pulled out the other chair across from her. "May I?"

"Sure. So do you normally pick up women this way, or you just thought you'd try out a new move?"

As Dave sat down on the chair, she could see the embarrassment on his face. "No, to both. This is my first time here. How about you?"

Jennifer noticed Laura sitting at the table with a man and gave her the thumbs up from the dance floor. Laura waved back at her. "Mine too, most likely the last though."

Dave watched Jennifer as she danced, grinning from ear to ear at them.

"Your friend seems to be having a good time."

"She works hard at it." Laura was feeling a little uneasy as she looked over at the handsome face watching her. She was glad to see the waitress on her way back with towel and drinks in hand.

"Here you go, hon." She handed Laura the towel with which she promptly used to wipe the table down. "That'll be $8.50."

Dave pulled out a ten Darrell gave him, from his shirt pocket, while the waitress placed the drinks in front of them. "Sorry, I have to charge that price, even for the non-alcoholic drinks, management rules."

"That's fine, keep the change." Dave said as the waitress was digging through her money tray for the change.

"Thanks, good lookin." The waitress said before she wandered off to the next table.

Dave and Laura sat staring at their drinks then he raised his glass for a toast. "Here's to two non-drinkers at a bar. Boy, do we seem to be an unlikely pair to meet in such a place."

Laura lifted her soda towards his. "Boy, Isn't that the truth? By the way my name is Laura Daniels."

Dave wiped his hand off on his jeans then reached across the table to shake Laura's hand. "David Martin, it's a pleasure to meet you ma'am and I am sorry about the spilled drink."

His handshake was firm and the warmth of his hand felt nice, but Laura felt uncomfortable with his touch and withdrew her hand. "The pleasure is mine, and you apologized once for the drink. That's enough, apology accepted, besides you've already made amends."

Jennifer popped up behind Laura from what seemed to be out of nowhere. Dave stood to give her seat back to her.

"No, no, sit. I'm not staying long. I just came by to see how my friend here is doing and get introduced to this good looker. Laura, are you going to introduce me, or what?"

Laura being a gracious woman introduced the two. "Jennifer this is David Martin, David, Jennifer Randall."

Dave spoke as they exchanged a handshake. "It's a pleasure to meet you ma'am."

Jennifer giggled then cranked her head up to listen. "Oh, I love this song. I have got to find a dance partner."

She grabbed Laura's arm and whispered in her ear. "He's cute. Good work, girlfriend."

As quickly as she appeared, she disappeared. Laura was left standing in the place where Jennifer had just left her. She raised her hand to her face. "Do you feel like you were just hit by a whirlwind?"

As they returned to their seats, Dave tried to be polite regarding his observations. "Something like that. She's a character isn't she?"

"Oh brother, that's an understatement."

"So how did you two become friends, I mean you two seem so different?"

"We work together. I've known her for a while, long before she became this "new and improved" Jen, as she likes to say. Sometimes, I think we pretty much tolerate each other's differences more than being friends with like interests."

Dave stared at his drink as he rolled it between his hands. "I've got a relative like that. Only a lot of times we don't even tolerate the differences very well. Actually, I'm here with him tonight." Dave was all of a sudden aware he had forgotten something, placed his hand on his forehead and exclaimed, "Oh man, I was supposed to be buying us another round of drinks. Now I don't even know where he is." He stood scouring the bar area where they had been, no Darrell. The dance floor was still filled with people, even though it was still the DJ playing the songs. There he saw Jennifer dancing up a storm. Continuing to look around, Dave saw his brother clinging to a woman who was just as drunk as Darrell. "Ah, there he is, still upright, but by the looks of him it doesn't look like he will be for too long." Content there was no immediate need to do anything more regarding his brother, Dave sat down. The sound of guitars tuning up could be heard while the DJ signed off and announced the band's return. They started in with a popular song. Clapping and whistle calls were heard from the audience. Swarms of couples crowded the dance floor. Now seemed like an opportune time as any for Dave to ask for his dance and he turned to Laura.

"Would you like to dance?"

"I'd love to only I don't know how to dance to that. I grew up dancing the twist, shimmy, the jerk and I feel like one right now." Laura sighed.

"They didn't do much couple dancing when we were growing up, did they? Nope. Our idea of a couple's dance was hanging on to each other and going round n' round in circles on a slow dance. When it's not so crowded down there I'll show you a couple of steps if you like?"

"I'd like that." She said smiling, hoping her outward demeanor was not betraying her inward feelings of complete awkwardness.

They both sat looking out over the sea of sweaty bodies on the dance floor below. Jennifer floated by smiling. Darrell had slipped and fallen, desperately trying to get up with the help of his dance partner. Several couples swished by, some talking, some looking lovingly into each other's eyes, and some appeared to be dancing as though they were dancing with a broom. Dave slapped his knee to the beat of the music. "They're good. They're real good."

Laura smiled in agreement and thought to herself. "Damn, I wish I wasn't so nervous. I wish I had paid attention when Matt was trying to teach me how to dance to this music. I wish I were home… No, I don't."

The band wound down the song. There was more clapping, hooting, and hollering from the audience. The lead singer announced, "We're going to slow way down now. We have a special song written by our own Sandi Lord. So take that special someone to the dance floor."

Dave rose, extending his hand to Laura. She received his hand in hers and they entered the dance floor. He placed his right hand gently yet firmly under her left arm and slid it around her back. His left hand enveloped her right hand in his.

"Okay, this is the only dance step I know. It's a simple two-step. Are you ready?"

Laura looked up at him, taking a deep breath, "Where you go I'll follow, try to anyway."

Dave pulled Laura closer to him. He could smell the faint odor of shampoo in her hair; he breathed in her fragrance. She could feel the warmth of his hand on her hand and against her back. The singer belted out the love ballad as they danced. The lyrics enchanted them as they glide across the floor.

"It's been such a long, long time.
You've been such a hard road to find.
How could I ever let you outta my sight,
now that I that I've found my one bright light.
Holding, holding you in my arms is a sweet dream come true,
a sweet dream come true.
You fill my days with hope and the hours pass by with soft memories of
your smile.
I count the minutes til' I see your face. As I travel the miles...
to hold you in my arms,
a sweet dream come true...."

Their faces almost touched and with this near touch, Laura lost the rhythm of the music. She stumbled and stepped hard on Dave's foot. "Oh, I'm so sorry."

They both stopped dancing. Dave took her hand back in his. "It's all right. Let's start again. Right foot back, there, that's it, you're doing great. Just don't think about it so much."

Laura tried not to look down at her feet. "That's funny, that's what my son told me when he tried to teach me."

Dave seized this opportunity to find out more about Laura. "How many children do you have?"

"Two, two boys."

"They have names?"

"Matt and Kyle."

Dave swung her around then pulled her back to him.

"And obviously they are old enough to know how to dance the two step?"

Laura was pleased with herself she did not stumble and fall. "Oh quite. Matt is twenty-one and Kyle just turned eighteen. Are you trying to distract me from counting and watching my feet?"

Dave leaned in close to Laura's ear and murmured, "Yep, is it working?"

Laura felt a shiver run down her spine. It was a good kind of shiver, but it made her feel uneasy, and she felt the need to take control of the conversation.

"Good, so far… How about you? Do you have any children?"

Dave responded beaming with pride. "Yes, ma'am. I am the proud father of two girls. Alicen and Trisha ages twenty and seventeen respectively."

Laura honed into Dave's usage of the word ma'am. "I like the fact that you're polite, but you can stop calling me ma'am now. I'm starting to feel like your elder."

"Yes, ma'am." Dave said with a smile as he twirled her around and dipped her backwards to the end of the song.

The band struck up the next song without skipping a beat. Dave was enjoying the closeness of the two of them dancing and tried his best to entice her into another dance.

"You did really good. Would you like to try another?"

Laura listened and watched the dancers around her. "I'd love to, but I think this one is a little too fast for my feet to keep up with. Your toes should be screaming relief."

Dave intertwined Laura's arm with his, they exited the dance floor and headed toward their table. "Not at all. I enjoyed every moment."

After they sat down at the table, Laura leaned forward so she could be heard. "Is it just me, or did they just get louder?"

"I think they just got a lot louder."

"What?"

Dave leaned forward, raised his hand, and with a soft gentle touch brushed her hair away from her eyes.

"Would you like to go out on the patio where we can talk?"

Laura's breath was all but taken away. It had been such a long, long time since a man had touched her that way. She swallowed barely able to speak. "I'd like that a lot." She said as she removed her coat from the back of her chair. They walked past the large dance floor, past two of the three bars towards the patio doors. As they walked through the hall, Jennifer caught sight of them leaving.

"All right, you go girl," she shouted as Dave and Laura exited the dance hall.

Jennifer's eyes were not the only ones watching them. Sean had been keeping track of Dave throughout the night. He began the evening in a surly mood, and with each passing drink, he became more belligerent, and drink he did.

The patio contained about fifteen to twenty tables. Japanese lanterns were strung around the perimeter. Four smudge pots were lit trying to warm the area. Two women were standing next to one of the lit pots trying to stay warm while smoking cigarettes. A man was leaning against the railing also smoking. At a corner table there was a couple cuddling, talking, and kissing. Laura began to put her coat on.

"Here let me help you with that." Dave assisted.

Laura gazed in wonderment at this gentleman before her. "Thanks, it's a lot colder than I thought it would be."

Dave removed her hair to the outside of her coat collar. He ran his fingers under her collar, sliding them toward the front of the coat, and pulled the coat together. "Is that better?"

Laura thought to herself, 'What a wonderful warm and kind face he has.' Then she composed herself and simply said, "Much."

Dave gazed into her eyes as though he was trying to find her soul thinking, 'Eyes that could steal a man's heart.'

"So," he said letting go of her coat, "should we continue with the obligatory question and answer session?"

They strolled closer to one of the smudge pots. Feeling the warmth of the fire, Laura looked intently at the face staring back at her. "Sure, I'll oblige by starting the inquisition. What do you do for a living?"

"I'm an electrician."

"Well, that was short and sweet. Do you like it? Do you own your own business, or work for someone else?"

"It's okay work, and it pays the bills. I work primarily in new construction except when the weather is too bad. When there are lay offs, I do a little side work of my own, repairing wiring in older homes, but I really don't like working the private sector. They are such pains in the…the, you know."

"How's that?" She said as she warmed her hands at the smudge pot.

"Well, you go do the job. It always seems to take too much time. Therefore, there's not much profit in it. Then by the time I get home they've called complaining that I didn't fix the problem, screaming about how they didn't pay *all* that money to still not be able to turn on their living room lights."

"Well, that sounds like lots of fun."

"The funny thing is I've gone back looking very serious, checked everything out, then put a new light bulb in, and viola there's light. At that point they are usually so embarrassed they slip me a little something for my time."

This initial conversation proved to be a pleasant surprise to Laura. She never thought she would even come close to having a good time.

"People are funny that way." She said.

Dave decided it was time to turn the table and find out more about this striking creature before him. "So, now it's your turn. What do you do?" He questioned.

"Well, basically I process the paper work for the Department of Motor Vehicles to transfer ownership on used cars sold at the dealership. I hate my job because of those cranky ol' people. Moreover, dealing with the State of California's rules and regulations, I swear, changes according to whom you're talking to. It's a virtual nightmare."

"You work with computers a lot don't you? Doesn't that help?"

"Most of my work is mountains of paperwork I do by hand. I work with computers. I like computers although they don't always like me. My boys each have one so I ended up knowing more about them than I ever wanted. I even went to school so I could learn more about them, like what to do when the new game one of them bought either doesn't work, or crashes the system."

"And what do you do when the game doesn't work, or crashes the system?"

Laura with a great deal of passion in her voice stated, "You throw the game away as fast as you can. I hate games. That's not why I went into debt on those blasted machines."

"You're a little passionate about this, aren't you?"

"Oh yeah, after the first time you pay someone a hundred dollars an hour to fix a problem, you get a little passionate about it. That's why Matt and I took the classes. Actually, we have gotten quite good at it. Unfortunately, now we seem to do a lot of pro-bono work. That doesn't bother me so much. It's just all the time and effort we will take to clean up someone's system and they are calling within a week because they crashed it again."

Dave thought a moment about the computer Josh had just given him. "I'm a little afraid to ask this, but seeings how you're the only computer expert I know."

"No expert here. I can take care of simple problems. Sorry, what's the problem you're having?"

"One of the guys at work gave me a computer for my girls. I think I've got everything plugged in right, but we just can't get the printer to work right."

"What's it doing?"

"Happy faces and strange looking symbols?"

Laura was relieved she recognized the problem. "Oh, that's easy. Just replace your printer cable. Make sure all the pins are straight first. If that doesn't work you may need to delete the printer in the printer settings then reinstall the drivers for it."

Dave imparted a look as though she just spoke to him in a foreign language. "The printer cable part I think I can handle, the rest sounds like Greek to me."

Laura rubbed her hands together and breathed on them trying to warm them up. Dave touched her hands.

"You're a little cold. Would you like to go back inside?"

Laura had been enjoying the conversation and did not want to leave. "No, I like it out here. It's peaceful, quiet. I like quiet. Something warm to drink would be nice. Coffee, two creams two sugars?"

Dave checked his shirt pocket for the money Darrell gave him and headed for the door. "I'll be right back. Now don't you go anywhere. You just stay there looking pretty. Just like that. Okay?"

Laura smiled out of the right side of her mouth. "Sure, I'll be right here."

She kept an eye on Dave as he left. She almost giggled to herself as she thought, 'Did he just say pretty? Thanks Jen for being so persistent. Thanks God.'

Sean noticed Dave coming in from the patio alone. He made his way down to the dance floor to get Ramón. Grabbing him by the shoulder he demanded, "Come on Ramón. You're going to play look out for me."

Ramón, spun away from a very drunk young woman he had been dancing with and whined, "Hey man. Not now."

Sean glared at him through his steel blue eyes. "Now. Ramón," he barked. He yanked Ramón away from the woman, she reached out for him and he back. "Hey, baby where are you going? The song's not over yet." The woman cooed.

Ramón, looking back over his shoulder as Sean escorted him toward the patio doors. "You stay right there sweet thing. I'll be right back. Damn it Sean! What's so important? I was just about to go home with that tight ass and get me some."

Sean stopped short of the double doors. "I told you. You are going to play look out for me. You remember that asshole from the job site?"

"Yeah, sure I do."

Sean peered through the glass in the door. Laura was still standing by the heater. "I'm going to play with his girlfriend and you're going to tell me when he comes back. You think you can handle that?"

There were times Ramón hated Sean's condescending tone, but he knew when Sean was on a mission there was no deterring him. With a frustrated tone in his voice, he acquiesced to Sean's demands. "What ever you say red."

Sean exited through the double doors. He walked straight over to where Laura was standing. Laura looked up expecting to see Dave. "That was qui…" She glared into Sean's cold eyes, and fear coursed through her body. "I'm sorry. I thought you were someone else." She turned away looking back at the heater, ignoring his presence, hoping he would just go away. Sean stood so close she could feel his warm breath and smell the liquor.

"Yeah, I know who you thought I was. You thought I was Mr. Clean, Mr. Right, Mr. Goody Two Shoes macho man. Didn't you pretty lady?"

Somehow, 'pretty lady' did not sound so nice now. Laura stood there afraid to move afraid to speak, praying for Dave to come back. Sean was intent in making Laura squirm.

"What do you want with an asshole like him when you could have a real man like me? Someone who could do you right and fuck you all night long. Make you scream, begging me to stop." He grabbed Laura's face with one hand and kissed her hard, shoving his tongue into her mouth. She tried to push him away to no avail. Sean pushed her head back still holding her face. "I bet that jerk never kissed you like that."

Ramón opened the door. There was a sense of panic in his voice. "Hey man, he's coming back. Let's get out of here."

"Later, pretty lady. There's a lot more where that came from. Sweet dreams." Sean said as he let go of Laura's face. If there could be a smile, which was pure evil, Laura just saw its face.

Dave recognized Sean and Ramón as they came back in from the patio area. He placed the two cups of coffee on the nearest table and immediately went through the doors to find Laura visibly shaken.

"Are you all right? What did they do to you? Laura?"

Laura made a poor attempted to compose herself. "I think I remember why I don't come to these kinds of places anymore. Do you know those guys? They seem to know you." Laura was still staring at the door where they had just exited, when Jennifer and her dance partner entered. As the door opened, Dave swung around. Startled at Dave's reaction, Jennifer blurted out, "Hey, what's going on out here?"

Laura tried to reassure Jennifer, "Everything's okay now; it was just a drunk harassing me, that's all."

Jennifer wrapped her arm around Laura. "Are you sure? You look white as a ghost. Come on let's go back inside where it's warmer and hopefully safer."

"That sounds like a good idea. You stay with Jennifer. I want to go make sure those guys left," Dave said still staring at the door. He then left to search out the place. Jennifer took Laura by the arm directing her back into the main hall, as Jennifer's escort followed.

"Guys? You didn't say anything about guys, plural. Are you sure you're all right?"

Laura patted Jennifer's hand. "I'm fine. I'm fine."

Sean and Ramón walked out to the truck acting as though nothing had happened. Ramón dug into his jacket pocket and pulled the wallet out that he had lifted from Dave earlier. It was a hand made leather wallet with the initials DM engraved on it. It had been a birthday gift from Trisha on his fortieth. Ramón pulled out $182 and stuffed it in his pants pocket. He thumbed through the wallet noting, driver's license, union card, and two pictures of Dave's daughters. Sean ripped the wallet out of Ramón's hands.

"You asshole! Why did you lift his wallet? Are you trying to get us caught before the job's even done?"

Sean threw the wallet on the ground while Ramón stared at him in confusion. "Man, you hit on his girlfriend, and your worryin' about me lifting his stinking wallet? I can't figure you out, man."

They climbed into the old beat up pickup truck. Sean opened the glove compartment to check on its contents. He pulled out a .45, checked to make sure it was loaded then placed it back in the glove box. Ramón sat in the passenger seat bewildered. "Shit, when did you put that in there?"

Sean ignored the question and backed the truck up. "Let's go by the site and see if they've increased security due to your five finger discount. I sure hope you got big bucks for this fuck up."

Ramón reached into his pocket to again count his find. "Nope, I think I did better with what's his face's wallet."

The remark angered Sean. He pressed the stick shift into first gear and slammed down the gas pedal. Dust and gravel flew everywhere.

Dave walked out the front door just in time to see the old white truck peel away. 'Good.' He said to himself and turned to go back inside when he saw something laying on the ground. He bent down and picked up a wallet. Then he checked his back pocket as though he expected to find it there.

"Damn it, when did that happen?"

He opened it up to find everything in tact except for the missing money. Dave placed the wallet back into his pant pocket. Standing in the cool of the night he looked up at the dark sky. It was difficult to see the stars through the parking lot lights. It had turned out to be a beautiful yet strange night. As he opened the heavy wood door, he could hear the sound of a sweet love ballad. He thought, 'It sure would be nice to end this night dancing with Laura.' The mere thought provoked soft smile across his face.

Sean and Ramón pulled up to the job site and turned off the headlights as they rolled in with the engine off. In the pit of darkness, they listened to the quiet of the night. A dog could be heard barking in the distance. From inside the site compound, the dome light of a car went on. The car door opened and a large dog at the end of a leash bolted out of the car restrained by a security guard. Sean pounded his hands on the steering wheel.

"Shit. Now I'll have to call and have the drop delayed til' the next phase." He turned his anger towards Ramón. "I told you, didn't I? I told you you'd cause nothing but trouble by taking these assholes tools. You're nothing but a fuck up. Why I keep you in this thing, I don't know." Sean started the truck up and put it in reverse. The dog and the guard were still heading towards them, so he placed the truck in first gear and headed down the road a ways before he turned the headlights back on.

Ramón did not like being held responsible for the set back. He spoke with a defensive, yet whiney tone in his voice. "Hey man! It's my connections that are going to make us rich. My people wouldn't have even talked to a gringo like you."

Sean stared straight ahead. "That may all change when they find out how helpful you've been, Ramón. That may all change."

The security guard arrived at the road to see the taillights of the truck disappear around the bend.

"Come on Serge, back to the car, report time."

It was a strange smell, a mix of alcohol, perfume, and sweat. The warmth of the room with the sounds of laughter and people trying to talk over the music made it seem as though nothing had just happened. Dave located Jennifer and Laura at a table away from the hordes of people. He snatched a chair from an adjacent table. "They left thank God. I see you finally got your cup of coffee, and the color has come back to your face.

Are you doing okay?" He placed the chair in front of Laura and took her hands in his. "I'm really sorry about that jerk bother'n you."

Laura tilted her head to one side, pondering his remark. "I appreciate your concern. I'm fine, but why are *you* apologizing?"

Dave leaned back in the chair releasing her hands. "I know them, I work with them and I must have done something to really tick them off."

Laura paused for a moment in thought as she realized how distraught this man was by the evening's events. "You're no more responsible for that 'jerk's actions than I am. Some people are just evil, and that man was evil. I don't think he needed a reason. I don't think he ever needs a reason. He gets off on watching the fear in people's eyes."

Darrell stumbled over to the table and almost fell on top of Dave. "There you are. I thought maybe you got lucky and left me here to fend for myself."

Dave obtained another chair and his brother plopped down. Darrell placed his head down on the table and passed out. "Laura, Jennifer, meet my brother Darrell. I think it's time to take the boy home so he won't miss his wedding tomorrow." Dave spoke with disgust then completely changed his tone to address Laura. "Would you do me a favor? Would you let me follow you two home? Just so I know that you get there safely, and I know those creeps aren't lying in wait to follow you home."

Jennifer would have been remiss if she had missed this opportunity to keep Dave and Laura together longer in hopes of her friend striking up a possible romance. "Oh, I think that would be a great idea. Don't you Laura?" she piped up.

Laura was tired from the night's turn of events. She could see no sense in arguing. "That would be fine. Now, would be as good a time as any."

Dave reached down and shook Darrell's shoulder. "Come on bro', time to go." Darrell struggled to his feet and Dave seized his right arm and placed it around his shoulder, assisting him out to his truck. Laura and Jennifer followed behind. He placed Darrell in the truck and fastened his seat belt.

"Now, *no* throwing up in my truck! Okay?"

There was no response from Darrell. Dave grabbed a handful his hair and pulled his head back. "Okay?"

Darrell struggled to open his eyes. "Okay! Roll the window down, I can't breathe."

Two cars pulled up by the truck. Jennifer yelled out the passenger window, "I live closest so how about we drop me off first." Dave gave her a two-finger salute, jumped in the truck and they all took off.

Twenty minutes later, Dave and Laura pulled up to her mobile home. She pulled into the driveway, and Dave stopped his truck behind her blocking the driveway. Laura fumbled for her keys in the dark, as Dave walked up to the stairs. "Is your light out?"

"Sorta. Actually, I have a short some where."

Finding the key, she placed it in the lock. Dave climbed up another step.

"Well, I am an electrician. I may be able to help, if you'd like."

Laura fumbled with the key until it turned the lock. She reached in to turn on the entry light. With the door cracked open, the light filtered onto the stoop. She turned to speak, but Dave interrupted before she could. "I'd like to do this for you."

Laura deliberately changed the subject. "You have a strange way of finding out where a lady lives. Did you have this planned?"

Dave climbed up the steps to the door where Laura was standing. He removed her glasses and placed them on top of her head. Then he cupped her chin in his hand, lifting her head up to look directly into her eyes. "There are a lot of things I'd like to find out about you, but no this part was not planned."

"This part?"

"I planned on dancing with you. Well, actually I almost chickened out when this strange thing happened. I was attacked by a lovely lady's chair and the rest is history."

"I was reaching for my purse."

Dave placed two fingers under the strap of her purse. "So I guess I have to thank your purse for our meeting."

Laura was almost unable to respond. "I guess so."

Dave was just about to ask Laura if he could give her a goodnight kiss when he heard the sound of Darrell throwing up. He turned towards Darrell's direction and shouted, "Ah man, you better not be hacking in my truck." Almost in a panic he returned to Laura, "I've got to get him home. Can I see you again?"

"Sure I'd like that."

The truck pulled away, soon to be out of sight. Laura entered her house and locked the door behind her. She took a moment to sit in the front room in her rocker to read from her bible and reflect on the evenings events before going to bed.

As Dave pulled up in front of his brother's house, he realized he forgot something. "Good move Dave, you forgot to get her telephone number. How are you supposed to call her? Driving up to her front door would be a little brash..., but doable. Come on little brother find your house keys it's time to pay the piper."

The Courtship

Eight o'clock Monday morning Dave entered the on-site office. Grace was hanging her coat up on the corner rack.

"Good morning Grace, is Nick going to be in this morning?"

Grace walked over to the coffee pot.

"Good morning Dave, Nick won't be in until around ten. He's at a meeting. Can I leave him a message?" She dumped the old grounds into the trash, placed a new filter in, and added new grounds.

Dave stood there thinking while he watched Grace. "No. Yes, tell him I really need to talk to him when he comes in."

Grace picked up the pot, which still contained the old coffee. "Is there a problem, Dave? Did you find more tools missing?"

"No, no Grace, it's nothing like that. Just tell him I need to talk to him. Okay?"

Grace emptied the old coffee down the drain in bathroom sink. This was a morning routine she could do in her sleep. "Sure, I'll tell him first thing." The phone rang and Dave decided there was no more that could be done at this time and left.

As he made his way back to his job destination, he looked around trying to find Sean and Ramón. They are nowhere to be seen. He joined Josh to finish the electrical on the house they had been working on. Josh was in the kitchen area pouring a cup of coffee from his thermos. "Would you like a cup? Joyce made extra. She even packed a cup for ya."

Dave was still deep in thought. He was wondering if what he was going to ask Nick to do was moral, or ethical. All he knew is he had to do something. Dave then noticed Josh was standing there waiting for an answer, replied, "Sure Josh, thanks."

"You've been mighty quiet this morning. What's going on?"

"Have you seen Sean and Ramón?"

"No, what do you want with them?"

"I had a run in with them on Saturday night."

"And?"

"I just want to keep an eye on those two. I think Ramón stole my wallet."

"I thought I saw you with it this morning at the donut shop?"

"Yeah, I found it later in the parking lot with no money, of course."

Josh held up his thermos to offer Dave some more coffee. Dave placed his hand over the cup indicating no more. Josh loved to hear gossip and this little tidbit only enticed him to hear more.

"Sounds like an interesting evening. What else happened? Come on give me the skinny, partner. You know this old man lives a boring life and the most excitement I get is hearing the stories of you youngin's."

Dave swirled the last of his coffee in his cup. "Darrell got drunk and passed out. I met and danced with a pretty lady that Sean managed to scare the hell out of."

"You sure know how to get to the short of a story. You care to expand on this, or are you just going to keep me in suspense?"

"Well my brother didn't break character. He was asshole extraordinaire, as usual. I don't even know if he went to Vegas like they were planning. I have no sympathy for Carroll if she married him. She's lived with him for three years. She knows what she's getting into."

Josh interrupted, "Darrell and Carroll. It sounds like a comedy team, or something."

"It is. Believe me it is, a tragic comedy."

"And what about this pretty lady you met?"

Dave's eyes lit up. "Don't know yet, but I think she's worth more exploration."

"So, you've got her number and you're going to call? Right?"

"Nope, didn't get her number."

Josh was exasperated at Dave's lack of attention to important details. "How the hell do you expect to find out more about this woman when you don't even have her phone numb…?"

Dave interjects, "I know where she lives."

"Dang, you move fast."

Dave almost had to laugh at Josh's reaction. "No, it's nothing like that. I followed her home to make sure she got there safely after Sean put a damper on the evening."

Josh's tone changed to concern. "What did he do, exactly?"

Dave bit his lower lip in thought. "I'm not exactly sure. Laura wouldn't tell me the details, but she was as white as a sheet after he left."

"Laura, nice name."

Through the years, their friendship had weathered through the good times and the bad. Josh was painfully aware when Dave was laboring over something of deep concern to him. He did his best to console his friend. "As far as those two miserable excuses for human beings, maybe they're gone for good. They were just extras hired to do menial work. I've not seen them around, and they are usually here by now."

"I don't think so Josh. I have a real bad feeling about them, a real bad feeling. I don't think I've seen the last of those two."

They sat in silence as they finished the coffee. Josh replaced the lid to his thermos as he searched his mind to think of something positive to say. "Well," he said, "it looks like today we will be able to work in peace."

The sounds of the construction site hummed on as Dave and Josh went about their work. Engrossed in the job, Dave did not notice Nick's return. Around ten-thirty, Nick hiked up to where Dave and Josh were working. He made a beeline straight over to where Dave was feeding electrical wire to a ceiling fan and inquired about the message he had left.

"Dave, Grace says you want to talk to me. What can I do for you?"

Josh watched as Dave and Nick talked, just out of his earshot. He moved closer pretending to work on a wall socket so he could hear what was being said.

"Dave, I don't think I can do that. I can't justify firing them on just a suspicion. I can't lay them off because there is obviously enough work for them. In fact, I have them working at the Chino Hills site to help them out." Nick objected, then searched his mind for a probable solution. "Maybe I can just keep them down there."

Since the very first day, Dave wondered why Nick would hire these two and now seemed to be as good as time as any to find out. "Nick, where did you find these guys? Why did you hire them? You've never hired trash like that before."

Under the circumstances, Nick felt obliged to explain. "It was part of a package deal with the owner of the company that's supplying the plumbing fixtures. He gave me a great discount if I'd hire his nephew to keep him off the streets. I'm sure they'd start screaming discrimination if I let Ramón go. Then I'd be tied up in court forever. Sean, I might have recourse with him. Let me work on this, and I'll get back with you. Okay?"

Nick had always been a fair man and a man of his word. Dave knew he would do his best to take care of the situation. "Thanks Nick," Dave said as he turned around to see Josh stooped at an already installed wall socket.

"Did you catch everything, or do I need to recap it for you?"

The embarrassment on Josh's face was all too apparent. He labored a little to stand, and then brushed off his pants.

"I caught the jest of it. I just hope they don't figure it's you that gets them the unemployment line."

Dave, more thinking out loud than to Josh, uttered, "Me either, but Nick is a diplomat. He'll handle it tactfully."

As they returned to work, the squeaky sounds of bad brakes could be heard at the front entrance. The initial shipment of plumbing fixtures had arrived.

***

Phase one of the housing development was almost done at the Chino Hills site. The landscaping crew needed to come in to put the finishing touches on the model homes. It was crucial to have all the debris around the models removed.

Sean and Ramón had just finished loading the truck for the third time and were heading towards the on-site trash bin. As they drove, the back tire on the driver's side hit a pothole and bounced the contents of the truck around. A cardboard box flew out and Sean stopped the truck to retrieve it, then continued on. There had been an uneasy silence between the two of them this particular morning. Sean had been in deep thought, playing over a conversation in his mind he had the night before. Approaching the trash bin, he turned to Ramón to let him know what was on his mind.

"I called Beto last night to let him know what was going on at the site. He said it didn't matter cuz' the delivery truck had been ceased at the Texas border. That's why they had delayed shipment to the Moreno Valley site. They were trying to get another shipment in via a different route. Unfortunately, that doesn't appear to be an option so they're going to wait until the second phase to do the drop. You got lucky, Ramón. I don't care if he is your Uncle. I don't think he would have taken your fuck up lightly."

Ramón stared straight ahead knowing this was a tenuous situation at best. One wrong word and he knew he would set Sean off.

"Yeah I know man. I talked to him too. I don't know what you said to him, but he chewed me up and spit me out. I didn't let him know about your goins on with Martin's girlfriend, so you owe me one."

Sean parked the truck next to the trash bin. They both began to throw trash from the truck into the bin when Sean paused to light up a cigarette. Sean's devious mind had a plan, but first he had to find out if it was viable.

"Ramón, did you see that blonde lady that was with Martin's girlfriend?"

"Yeah, what about her?"

"Have you seen her there at the club before?"

Ramón could see Sean had a very specific purpose with his questions, and he did not even want to know where this was going. He knew it meant it was going to require him to do something he did not want to do.

"Yeah, she's there all the time. Why?"

Then came the punch line Ramón had been waiting for.

"I want you to get close to her."

Ramón's leg started to shake at the thought. "Ah man, that old woman?"

"I didn't realize you had standards."

"I've got standards, and I draw the line at old women."

"I'm not asking you to fuck her, just get some information from her. Anyway, I've seen you pay for whores older than her."

Ramón picked up a piece of trash from the truck and threw it at Sean in play. He dodged it easily, laughing. Ramón had a tone of frustration and whine in his voice as he asked, "What do you need from that old broad?" Now there was an intensity in Sean's face and he paused to word his response. "Just some information, that's all you need to know."

Ramón knew at this point the conversation had ended for Sean had returned to emptying the truck of its contents. As they headed back to the model home area, Ramón remembered something his Uncle Beto told him the night before.

"Sean, I forgot to tell you, Uncle Beto said Juan's wife has been driving him crazy asking about Marie. I guess she hasn't phoned them in months. The Mamacita is starting to worry something has happened to her little girl. I know you know where she is, her being your girl and all. So, you had better call her and tell her to call home, man. Otherwise they'll send the goon squad up to find her and take her home."

Sean's hands gripped the steering wheel of the truck so hard his knuckles turned white. He did not bother to hide the anger in his voice. "I told you before she is not my girl. Not anymore, not after she ran scared. She thought immigration was going to deport her, so she was going to start talking. She would have too if I hadn't found her that nanny job in Chicago. She really loves those kids. So, she won't do, or say anything now, not if she wants to wipe those brats' noses tomorrow. All right, yeah, I'll call her, but I don't know if she'll even talk to me. She says she hates my guts. Anyway, the people she works for have restricted calling on their phones. No toll calls so she has to walk to a pay phone to make a call. Marie said it's about an hour's walk. You tell your Uncle what I told you. Remember, she wanted to get away from those people down there so if she calls, she calls, no guarantees. You got that?"

Ramón did not expect a long dissertation on Marie, but then again Sean was known for his tangents. He shrugged his shoulders. "Yeah sure, no skin off my back. Marie always was a pain in the ass. She always had to do things her way. Suppose on her pay, she can't afford a cell phone. No problem, I'll tell him."

Sean felt confident he had fed Ramón just enough information to keep him and his Uncle from asking too many questions. He parked the truck next to the model home and worked in silence while trying to think of a plan to put a permanent end to any further inquiries, at least any inquires directed towards him.

***

Another day's work done, Laura and Jennifer were leaving work, heading towards their cars. Jennifer arrived at her car first.

"See you tomorrow. Oh yeah, that's right, you're taking the rest of the week off. How did you manage to get the week of Christmas off? Why didn't you take today off too?" Jennifer asked.

Laura stopped by Jennifer's car. It had seemed like an eternity since the last time she had taken a vacation. Life and her job had beaten her down, and she was just plain exhausted. "I haven't taken any vacation time in two years. So, basically, I begged. I just had to make sure all the weekend sales were logged in and submitted to Sacramento. They don't have anyone else who can, or will do the desk when I'm gone."

Jennifer opened her car door and threw her purse on the passenger seat. She understood all too well the problems at work. "I think everyone's desk is like that. Do you have any special plans this week?"

Laura shifted her purse and bag of empty plastic containers from one arm to the other while she fumbled for her keys. "No, nothing special. Just some last minute Christmas shopping, like buying a tree. Matt talked me into it again this year. I keep wanting to get an artificial, but he says that wouldn't seem like Christmas. In fact, I'm going over to pick one out now. Matt said he'd help put it up tonight. You want to come with me?"

Jennifer reluctantly turned Laura's offer down as she plopped herself behind the steering wheel of her car. "Can't, I have to go over to my brother's house. They invited me over for dinner. They worry a lot about me since my divorce. You're coming back for the office party aren't you?"

Wishing she did not have to attend, she politely stated, "Wouldn't miss it." She paused for a moment as she thought about last Sunday. "By the way thanks for keeping your end of the bargain. You never said if you enjoyed the services, or not."

Jennifer, as serious as she ever could allow herself to get, says, "It was nice. Only I felt like I should have gone to confession first."

"It wouldn't hurt, you know."

"Probably not. Hey, have you heard from that Dave guy yet?"

Laura felt she had to pull the reins in on this conversation. So, she reminded Jennifer of the time line. "It's only been a couple of days

Jen. Give the man a break. He has a life, kids, and a job. If he's interested he'll come around."

"I just don't know how you can be so 'laze fare' at your age."

"I'm not looking, and I've never been looking. You are, that's why you're so impatient."

"Probably so. Just keep me up to date if anything happens. Okay? I've got to get going. See ya Thursday."

Pulling into the driveway, Laura noticed there were not any lights on in the house. She entered from the side door and found a note from Matt on the kitchen counter.

Dear Mom,

Work called me in. Will be home around midnight. Took Kyle to Meagan's house.

He said he'd be back home Xmas Eve. Sorry about the tree. I'll help you with it tomorrow.

XOX

Matt

Laura placed the note back down on the counter talking to herself, "Swell, one six foot tree, one five foot four woman. Whelp, I need to go to the grocery store so I better go put the grubs on if I'm going to pull that thing in tonight." Laura changed her clothes, untied the tree from the top of her car, and dragged it into the house to the living room floor. She stood there looking at the tree then at the tree stand. Newt as curious as ever, went about smelling the new arrival.

"Nope, I think not Newt. The rest will just have to wait until tomorrow. I leave you in charge to protect the homestead while I run some more errands."

She walked into the kitchen to wash her hands. Again, the sink and counter were full of dirty dishes. She exclaimed, "You'd think they both had broken arms." Newt jumped up on the counter looking for food. Laura opened the cabinet looking for a can of soft food for him. There was none. "Guess you'll just have to eat some dry food." She placed some in his dish and he snubbed it. "Okay, okay I'll go to the store now."

Laura took an over size sweater and pulled it on over the old t-shirt then snatched up her keys. First, she stopped to pick up some wrapping paper for the few gifts which were going under the tree, then made a beeline for the grocery store which was away from the mall so the traffic was light, and there were plenty of parking spaces. Once inside she took out her list, checking off the items as she placed them in her basket.

Rolling the crippled cart towards the check-out stand, she remembered she did not get any creamer. At the dairy section, she stood on her tiptoes trying to reach the last container of half and half. A hand came up from behind her and picked up the container just out of her reach. "Can I help you with that ma'am?" This was that voice, she knew this voice.

Dave was standing behind her holding the last of the creamer, smiling mischievously. Laura glared at Dave then at the creamer.

"Um yes, you can help by giving me what you're holding in your hand, Sir."

"Sir is it now. Hm, I don't know. I think I need this," he held the container out so he could read what it said, "this half and half."

"You do, do ya? I figured you to be a man who drank his coffee black."

Dave placed the container under his arm.

"I do, but I was thinking of changing my ways."

"Well you picked a heck of a time to change your ways. Now come on give me my creamer."

Laura reached for the container, but Dave pulled it away. Seeing the reaction he was getting, Dave teased even more.

"No, I like cream in my coffee. I just can never figure out how much sugar goes with it. It always ends up too sweet."

"Pour from the box do you?"

"How did you know?"

"I have boys, remember? I keep telling them spoons work really good for measuring sugar."

"A spoon?"

"Yes, a spoon. It's a real handy little utensil." Dave placed the creamer down in her basket then he teased with her some more. "Maybe you can show me how it's done sometime."

"Maybe."

Dave checked out the contents of her basket. He noted creamer, butter, coffee beans, sugar, cat food, and a pre-made bundt cake.

"I see you don't go in much for the made-to-taste like the real thing products."

Laura started pushing her crippled cart down the isle. "So, are you checking to see if I'm one of those health food nuts? I'm not. I like dark greasy coffee beans, real cream, real sugar, and real butter."

Dave was not able to leave this one alone. "And real men?"

Laura abruptly stopped her cart. "Why Mr. Martin are you flirting with me?"

"I'm a little rusty, but yeah. Is it working?" Dave said with a little boy quality.

It had been a very long time since a man flirted with her. She almost did not know what to say. Laura stammered, "Yes, you've managed to get me quite flustered. So… what are you doing in this neck of the woods? You don't live around here do you?"

Dave could see he had embarrassed Laura. Not wanting to scare her away, he stopped his teasing.

"No, I dropped Trisha off at choir practice. The churches are having a combined Christmas show."

Laura started to push the cart up an aisle, making her way to the checkout stand. She took her time, looking at items on the shelf, pretending she had more shopping to do. She had hoped she would see Dave again, and she did not want this unexpected meeting to end.

"Yes, I know I'm going to the concert tomorrow night, but that doesn't explain why you're wandering around picking up strange women in grocery stores."

"Actually, I was at the gas station when I saw you pull in, and you're anything but strange. You say you're going tomorrow night? Would you like to accompany me to the concert, then a small get together afterward?"

"I, uh, you, uh, you baffle me. I don't think I've ever been pursued. You are pursuing me aren't you?"

"Yes ma'am. Would you please say 'yes' so I can stop holding my breath?"

"Yes sir, I would be delighted."

Dave checked his watch and realized he only had ten minutes before choir practice was to let out, and Trisha would be waiting to be picked up. He took hold of Laura's hand. "Thank you. You won't regret this, promise. I've got to go now. I'll pick you up around six-thirty?"

"That'll be fine. You do remember where I live, right?"

"Oh yeah, it's etched in my memory forever."

Laura entered the quick cash lane, and Dave left the store. As she stood there, Laura could see her reflection in an overhead mirror. Normally she would turn away, but this time she looked long and hard trying to see what had attracted this handsome man to her. She searched her image to no avail and shrugged her shoulders.

The cashier took her items, ran them through the scanner giving her the total. "That will be $17.83 ma'am." Laura continued to stare into space. "Ma'am, $17.83?" Laura paid the cashier then drove home to her empty house.

Matt and Laura spent the better part of the afternoon putting the tree up. He could get her to giggle and laugh while recanting stories from Christmases past with every decoration they hung. Every year they would each buy, or make a new decoration to add to the tree. This year Matt bought a Raggedy Ann and Andy.

"Mom, I bought this one in hopes that by next Christmas you'll have someone special to share it with."

Laura held the ornament in her hand. A small smile lit her face as she hung it on the tree. She turned to her son giving him a loving hug. "You're such a sentimentalist. Some woman is going to be very lucky to have you as a husband. I wonder what Kyle's contribution will be this year, a goat's head?"

Matt knew his mother's sarcasm was really hiding her concern. "Don't worry about Kyle. He'll come around. He's just going through a phase. He doesn't even believe in all that satanic stuff. He just knows these girls he hangs with are into it, and he is very into girls."

"I find it all just so very disgusting and scary. Who knows what kind of trouble he could get himself into?"

Matt decided the conversation had turned too serious for his liking. He put on a Christmas tape, one that had been around since he was just a kid. Laura sat down in the rocker and giggled, "Oh boy. The Chipmunk Christmas, where did you ever find that?"

Matt was so very proud of his rediscovery. "It was at the bottom of my sock drawer, bring back memories?"

Laura leaned back in her rocker. The same one she used to rock her babies to sleep. "Sure does. That's when Christmas still had magic in it."

Matt could see a glow in his mother's face as she remembered days past. "It still can, Mom. I want you to have a good time tonight. Okay? I wish I could go to the concert with you, but… work. Actually, I really wish I could stick around to meet your date."

The rocker stopped. The words had sounded so odd coming out of her son's mouth.

"Date? Yeah, I guess this is an official date. I think you'd like him. If things go well you'll meet him, eventually."

Matt and Laura hung the last of the decorations on the tree. As they did, he checked the time on the clock now hidden by the tree.

"Well, that's the last of them, Mom. I have to go get ready for work now and you for you date. Go get'em tiger woman."

Laura peered around the tree, noting it was only three o'clock. "Yeah right, it's never taken me three hours to get ready for anything."

Matt lovingly wrapped his arm around her shoulder. "So maybe this will be a first. Go ahead pamper yourself, you deserve it."

***

Singing could be heard from the shower. Alicen banged on the door trying to get her father's attention.

"Dad, hey Dad, Trisha and I are leaving now. We'll meet you at the church. Okay?"

Dave rinsed the soap from his hair and face, grabbed a towel, and wrapped it around him. He opened the door a crack and stuck his head out. Steam from the bathroom wafted out in the hallway. Alicen backed up and swatted at the air.

"Hey you're going to make my hair frizz! Boy, you sure are in a good mood. Singing country music in the shower, and I didn't even know you listened to country. This must be some woman. I can't wait to meet her."

Dave raised his eyebrows and gave her his mischievous smile.

"Give your old Dad a kiss and get out of here. I'll see you there. Break a leg Trish." He yelled out towards the front door.

Trisha ran up to give her Dad a quick kiss. "Love ya Dad. Come on Alicen I don't want to be late."

After the girls left, Dave remained wrapped in just the towel. He shaved, without using a mirror and then took out a rarely used after shave cologne. Splashing the cologne on his face, he cringed. He picked up the bottle and talked to it. "Damn, I forgot how much you sting."

With the bottle to his nose, he sniffed its contents. "Hmmm, you do smell nice though." He wiped an area dry on the mirror. Looking at his reflection, he saw a middle-aged man with a receding hairline. He backed up a little. "Not bad for an old man."

Dressed in black trousers, a white buttoned down shirt and a black sports jacket he took one last look in the mirror. He removed a brush from the drawer and combed his hair back, giving himself a wink at the mirror. He snatched up his truck keys from the counter and headed for the store. There he bought a single red rose with a sprig of baby's breath. Placing it on the passenger's seat, he turned the ignition starting the truck and flipped his way through the radio stations until he found a country station.

Laura decided to take Matt's advice and pamper herself. She used a henna rinse on her hair giving it red highlights. This time she curled her hair and put makeup on. Donning a hunter green sweater-skirt set with black hose, she searched her closet floor for her black high heels. Having found them, she blew the dust from them. Then with a sock from her drawer, she buffed them out. Sitting on the bed, she put her shoes on then stood before the full-length mirror. She promptly sat back down on the bed and sighed, "I'm too old for this." The phone rang. She reached over to the nightstand and picked it up.

"Hi Jen… No, he's not here yet… I told you what I was wearing… It looks fine. It looks as good as it gets…what do you mean that's no attitude to take…I know, but the truth is, it is as good as…" There was a knock at the front door. "Jen… he's here. I have to go now. My fate is sealed…. Jen, I have to go. Bye." Laura hung the phone up and quickly looked in the mirror. She closed her eyes for a moment, took a deep breath, and then exhaled, "Onward to door number one." She opened the door to see a grinning face. Dave was holding his right hand behind his back.

"You look beautiful."

He presented her the rose from behind his back. Laura graciously accepted, "Thank you, come in, please. I'll go put this in water." She promptly headed towards the kitchen to place the flower in a bud vase. Dave followed, objecting to her plans for his gift. "No, no, I want you to wear it."

Laura inspected the long stem rose and held it up to her dress.

"It's kind of long don't you think?"

Dave removed a knife from a wood block set sitting on her counter. He cut most of the stem off then proudly presented it to her again.

"Here, now you go find something so I can pin it to this pretty dress."

Laura departed into the bathroom, opened drawer after drawer looking for a pin

"I feel like I'm going to the prom, getting pinned and all. Here we go, this will do." She said as she pulled out a large safety pin.

Dave leaned against the bathroom doorway watching her search through the drawers.

"Didn't go to the prom. Damn, you're pretty."

Laura handed him the rose with the pin.

"Don't you ever go get your eyes checked!"

"I'm afraid I'm going to stick you. You better do it." Dave said as he fumbled with the pin.

She took the pin back and quickly fastened the rose to her sweater, looking in the mirror to make sure it looked alright.

"Why didn't you go to the prom? I thought everyone went to at least one prom."

Dave was still staring at her as she attempted to make the safety pin less noticeable.

"It's a long story. I'll tell you all about it later, but we need to get going."

They walked into the living room. Laura removed her coat from the closet, and he helped her put it on. As he shut the door behind them, he held his right arm out for Laura to take. Arm n' arm they strolled to his truck. Dave opened the door for her, but she hesitated at the truck door trying to figure out how she was going to traverse the step and still be lady like.

"Hold on just one minute. Let me get something out of the back of the truck." Dave said as he assessed the problem.

He opened up the tool chest and removed the toolbox. He placed it under the side step and took her hand. "There you go." Laura climbed in adjusting her skirt as she did so. He closed her door then put the toolbox back. Dave, positioned behind the wheel, considered Laura's dilemma.

"I never thought about dresses and the truck. Guess I need to go get a step stool." As he started up the truck, Country music came blaring out the speakers. He adjusted the volume down then engaged the stick shift in first gear. With the truck in gear, they began their first date.

The church was always crowded at Christmas time, but tonight it was extraordinarily cramped. They worked their way towards the front where Alicen was saving some seats for them. Squeezing past a couple at the end of a pew, they found their seats. Alicen stood and gave Dave a kiss on the cheek. She reached over to shake Laura's hand.

"Hi, I'm Alicen and you must be Laura."

"It's a pleasure to meet you, Alicen."

They sat as the concert began. It was well-done, but long. Dave beamed as Trisha did a short solo. Laura was feeling a little uncomfortable meeting Alicen and Trisha on their first date. The concert ended, and the people filtered out. Alicen turned to her father.

"I'm going to go back stage and get Trisha. I'll be right back. So, don't go anywhere yet, okay?" She turned to Laura. "I want her to meet Dad's new girl."

Laura glanced up at Dave. "New girl? I don't know if I'm ready for this."

Dave took her by her arm. "It will be fine. They are both good kids. They'll like you just fine."

"I don't know. I'm treading on their territory."

Alicen came back with Trisha in tow.

"Trisha this is Laura, Dad's date."

"Oh so you're the one Daddy's been grinning ear to ear about. Nice to meet you. Daddy, did I sound all right up there? I was so nervous."

"Not as nervous as some of us sitting down here." Laura quipped.

Trisha and Alicen looked at each other and giggled. Dave held his daughter's hand.

"You sounded beautiful, just beautiful."

"Thanks, but I knew you'd say that. What did you think?" She said turning to Laura.

"You were great, you were wonderful. I always wished I could sing. Instead, I sound like a cat run over by your Dad's truck."

Trisha giggled again then pulled herself up to Dave's ear. "I like her." She stepped back. "Dad, I know you wanted us to go to Josh's house, but it's so boring there. There's nothing to do. The only time there's any excitement is when Uncle Darrell is there, and I can pass on that. So I was wondering if it would be all right if Alicen and I went with a bunch of kids from the church Christmas caroling, and afterwards we want to go to get a bite to eat. Would that be okay? Please Dad? Please?"

Laura glared at Trisha with astonishment. "Did she just say all of that with one breath?"

Dave responded to his daughter's request. "Sure, but be home by midnight." Trisha gave a big, "Yes!" Then she thought about the time limit. "Midnight? Like you'll be there."

Dave raised his hand to his ear as though talking in a phone. "There's always a phone nearby, and if I am not home I will be calling the house. So you better be there, or you're grounded. Understand?"

Trisha acted disappointed, "Yes sir."

No sooner said and done, they are both gone. Dave turned to Laura. "You should see her when she's really wound up."

"Girls giggle a lot don't they?"

"Yeah, especially those two. Come on let's go. You must be starved by now, and Joyce always has enough food to feed a small army."

It was a small, but nice house in Corona. Josh and Joyce were warm and gracious hosts. After the obligatory introductions with the question and answer session, Dave and Laura sat in the front living room. The rest of the guests were talking and eating in the kitchen, or outside playing a game of darts. An artificial log burned in the fireplace. Laura sat on the floor in front of the sofa with her plate on the coffee table. Dave had plopped himself in a plush chair across from her. He had already finished his plate of food and set it on the table. Joyce entered the room and picked up the plate as though she had radar.

"Do you want anymore? There's plenty. I'll be more than happy to get you a second helping."

Dave patted his belly. "No thanks Joyce. Really, I'm full. It was delicious as usual. In fact I think you out did yourself this time."

Joyce beamed with pride. "Why thank you, Dave. How about you, Laura, can I get you something?"

Trying to look ladylike, Laura picked at her food.

"No thanks, Joyce, I'm fine."

Joyce realized she was intruding, "I'll just leave you two alone so you can get better aquatinted." Then she vanished into the kitchen.

Laura took a sip of her coffee. "She's a nice lady, a mother hen, but a nice lady."

"Joyce is the salt of the earth. She's the kind of woman that should have had eight kids. Instead, she has three dogs, two cats, a canary, a well-fed husband, and one son who could never do any wrong in her eyes. Don't get me wrong Justin is a good guy. He's just not as close to sainthood as Joyce would lead you to believe."

Laura stabbed a piece of ham with her fork as she tried to come up with something diplomatic to say. "Mothers tend to do that more than Dads."

"Not all mothers."

Laura quickly removed the fork from her mouth, leaving the piece of ham dangling on the end.

"Ouch, did I hit a raw nerve?"

Dave's past had reared a passionate head. So, he tried to discount it, by saying, "It was a long time ago."

"Does this have something to do with not going to the prom?"

"No, not really. I was just too busy being drunk and hanging out with my buddies to be bothered with proms and all that silly nonsense."

"Silly?"

"I don't think so now, but back then I was a rowdy young man to put it politely."

"So what straightened you out?"

Dave leaned forward with his forearms resting against his thighs.

"It's a long and not so pretty story. Are you sure you're ready to hear it?"

"Fire away. I think this is called the getting to know each other, discovery process," she said as she sat back trying to get comfortable.

Dave let out a big sigh then began to regale his life's story.

"Okay, here goes. I enlisted in the Army at 18 and started active duty on my 19th birthday. Boy, were my parents happy to see me go. I was always in trouble for one thing, or another. Usually it was drug or alcohol related. While in the service, I couldn't do drugs unless I wanted to be court marshaled, but I sure would drink myself into a stupor. Even though I was drinking heavily, I did well in the service. I was promoted quickly. I had just received my commission as a Warrant Officer when I met Christine. We were two of a kind Christine and I. We drank and partied all the time. That was here in the States, and I was due to be shipped out to Germany. I thought we were in love, so we got married, and the following month we went to Germany. I don't think we were there more than three months, and she announced she was pregnant. I was twenty-one years old with more than three years left on my tour. I was no more ready for a family than to be Commander n' Chief. When Alicen was born, she was the most beautiful miracle I had ever seen. I held this tiny little living being in one hand, and I decided right then and there that was it; I wasn't going to drink anymore. I wanted more than anything to watch her grow up and live long enough to walk her down the aisle and bounce grandchildren on my knees. I knew if I kept going the way I had been, I was a dead man. Unfortunately, Christine's venture into sobriety didn't last. Alicen was about two or three, I re-upped for four more years, and we came back to the States for about six months. This was the first time my parents met my wife and child. They hated Christine. She spent the entire week at their house locked in the bedroom. She wouldn't even come out and eat with the family. I suspected she was drinking again, but I never caught her at it. We went back to Germany, and that year Trisha was born. In 1981, during the Cold War, we were stationed near the East German border. They called it the 'Fulda Gap'. My cavalry unit was always being called out on alert. I was gone anywhere from a couple of hours to a week out in the field. This one time I was called out, we were only there over night. I came home the next morning around ten-thirty to find Alicen and Trisha sitting at the coffee table with bowls of cereal and milk spilled everywhere, watching cartoons. As soon as they saw me, they came running all excited and yelling, "Daddy's home, Daddy's home." I picked

Trisha up and she was sopping wet. Her nose was running, and she looked like she had been crying for hours. I made some remark like, "Has Daddy's little girl been crying?" Alicen piped up, "I tried to wake Mommy up, but she wouldn't wake up so I help sissy out of bed and made her beck-fst." She was so proud of herself. I asked her if Mommy was still sleeping, thinking something had to be terribly wrong. I thought maybe she had overdosed. She put her little finger to her mouth and goes, "Shh, Uncle Brad is sleeping too."

Laura stared at Dave in horror. "Oh my God, what did you do?"

"I opened the door and saw my wife with some Airman puke, passed out on the bed. I closed the door and called my commander to report the situation. I stipulated that someone needed to get there real fast because if either one of them had woke up, I didn't know what I would have done. The Airman was brought up on charges of adultery. Family services were called in to investigate child neglect. They found her unfit, and I sent her back to the States. I stayed in Germany till the end of my tour. I hated the idea of day care, but they had great schools, and day care was on the base. I wanted to keep as far away as I could from that woman. I was actually scared of what I might do if I saw her. Once I was back in the States, I filed for a divorce and sole custody of the girls. It was granted uncontested."

Laura was flabbergasted at his last statement. "Didn't she want to see her own kids?"

Dave continued, "She wrote almost everyday the first month. Then it dwindled to once a week, once a month, then on birthdays and Christmas. I kept the letters for the longest time. One day I pulled them out and read them. They were incoherent, the babblings of a drunk. She filed for visitation rights once. I agreed she could see them whenever she wanted, as often as she wanted. I'd even help her find a place walking distance from us and get her a job. My only stipulation was she had to submit to random drug and alcohol testing once a week for three months first. I'd pay for it so she couldn't use that as an excuse. That was the last I heard about her visitation rights."

"Didn't the girls ever ask about her?" Laura asked, still puzzled.

A deep sadness overcame him as he thought about how hard the girls took their mother's absence. "I had told the girls, mommy was very sick and she had to go away where hopefully she would get better. When that didn't work, I told them just enough of the truth so they would understand. I always told them it wasn't their fault. That they were wonderful, loveable little girls and it was just that some people didn't have the ability to love anyone more than they needed the drink. She started calling us again about two years ago. I kept arranging to meet with her, but every time she was a no show. Then one day she appeared at my front door with a little boy around six or seven in tow. She looked awful. I could barely recognize her she looked so old and haggard. The taxi pulled away about the time I realized who she was. She was still a drunk and had been drinking heavily. The kid didn't look right. He was probably born with that fetal alcohol syndrome. I felt sorry for the kid. She said her old man had thrown her and the kid out and she didn't have anywhere to stay. I wasn't about to let her stay with us. So, I called a local shelter. I drove her and the kid down there and that's the last I've seen or heard from her. The girls never knew she was there, and at this point I don't see what good it would be for them to know."

Laura was overwhelmed with the sadness of these girls' lives.

"Under the circumstances I fully agree. From what I've seen of your girls, you have done a great job raising them. They seem to adore you." She said.

He beamed, "Yeah they do, don't they?"

Laura played with the remaining food on her plate.

"I always find it astounding that even when a kid has a parent who abandoned them, beats them, or sexually abuses them they still decide to be good people. Then there are those who find every excuse in the book to justify doing wrong."

Dave sat back in the oversized chair with his hands clasped behind his head.

"I have a feeling we aren't talking about my girls anymore."

"No, I'm talking about Kyle my youngest. He's the type of young man if he came courting your daughter I would expect you to greet him at the door with a shotgun in hand. I'll tell you what; I'll take my tragic story over yours any day. He has nothing to complain about, but complain he will."

Dave was rather surprised by Laura's bluntness about her son. "Kind of harsh on the kid aren't you?"

"Oh no, he's into this Gothic, devil worship, wicken bullshit. Forgive my mouth, but that's what it is."

"Where's his Dad?"

"He died when Kyle was around eight."

"How did that happen, if you don't mind me asking?"

As difficult as it was for Laura, she decided it was only right she let Dave know as much as she could. "He was working on a tilt up. The scaffolding wasn't secured properly, and he didn't have his secondary belt on. I don't know if it just gave way or what, but he fell forty feet to the ground. He was in a coma for two days. I was supposed to make a decision regarding the life support the following day. I don't know if it was fortunate or unfortunate, but I didn't have to make that decision. He died during the night."

Dave moved to sit down on the floor next to her, taking her hand. "I'm sorry about your loss."

"That's okay, that's ten years past now."

"Is that when Kyle started acting out?"

Now she had to deal with the more recent past. The past still stuck in her throat when she spoke of her father.

"No, it started after my Dad died. He was real close to my Dad. They were planning this deep-sea fishing trip. That's all I heard about for months. Matt, Kyle, and my Dad, the men were going fishing for big game. Only Dad died of a stroke before the big day came. I think Kyle feels he's been short changed in life. Matt on the other hand feels lucky he got to know and love his grandfather and is thankful for what time he had with him. It all boils down to a matter of perspective, doesn't it?"

"Sometimes they don't seem to understand that life isn't fair. Never has been, never will be… You know I find us even more ironic than last Saturday. Here we are two non-drinkers, church going, bible-believing people (which certainly is not politically correct this day and age) who both have tragic first marriages, who meet in a bar we never go to. Go figure, do you think it's fate, or God's handy work?" Dave winked.

Josh entered the front room. "Hey you two! You're looking way too serious in here. How about you two joining us in a game of darts? I need some real competition Dave."

Laura quipped, "Well you certainly aren't going to get it from me."

Dave helped her up from the floor. "Nah, you'll probably whoop his sorry behind. He just thinks he's good, but he and I both know he's all talk."

They played darts until it became too cold, then they said their Thank you's and Good-byes. As Dave drove Laura home, he took special notice of the time. The clock read 12:04. He picked up his car phone and hit the speed dial to call home. With the speaker on, Trisha's sleepy little voice squeaked out of the speaker.

"Hi Daddy."

Dave smiled at the thought that Trisha knew it was him calling.

"I was just checking. I'll be home in a little while. Okay Pumpkin?"

"Okay, I'll probably be asleep when you get here. Love ya. Bye." Trisha said through a yawn.

The line went dead, and he fumbled in the dark to hang up the phone back on its receiver. He turned into the mobile home park and pulled up in front of Laura's home. There was not a single outside light on at the front of the unit. Dave again broached the subject of the needed electrical repair.

"It really bothers me you don't have any lights. I can come by tomorrow when you get off work and see if I can fix the problem."

Laura squirmed at the prospect. She did not like being a charity case, or owing people favors.

"It'll be dark then. You can't work in the dark can you?"

"The dark can be a problem, but I'm taking tomorrow off, actually the rest of the week off, so if one of your boys are home I could come over early and have it all done by the time you get home." He offered.

Laura thought about the proposal for a moment then decided an answered prayer was an answered prayer. Just because it did not fit her idea of how it should be answered did not mean this was not God's remedy to her problem. She acquiesced with a tone of gratitude in her voice. "That won't be necessary. I'll be home. Great minds think alike. I also took this week off."

Dave was pleased. Not only could he help Laura, but he also had a way to see her again. He set a time before she tried to back out of his offer.

"Great. I'll be here at eight o'clock."

Laura, looking forward to at least one day when she could sleep in, exclaimed, "Eight o'clock!?!"

"Okay nine."

She considered his counter; it seemed silly for her to make it difficult on him. "I can do nine."

Dave came around to the passenger's side of the truck. He grabbed hold of Laura by the waist and helped her down. Just inches away from each other they stood next to the truck under the streetlight. Dave gently held Laura's hands in his.

"I had a really good time. You're great company. Thanks for coming with me tonight."

Laura warmly greeted Dave's gaze. "It was nice. It was very nice. Once I got over being nervous, I had a good time. You're an easy person to be around. You're not pretentious, and I like that."

Dave leaned forward to give Laura a soft short kiss on the mouth. "Dittos." He encircled her arm with his and escorted her to the front door, waited for her to unlock it, and then enter inside. She turned around to see he was still standing in the doorway holding the door open. "Come here." He beckoned. She moved up to where he was standing. Dave touched her face then moved his hand to the back of her head. He drew her closer and kissed her again. "Just wanted to make sure I didn't imagine the first time."

Laura fumbled for some words, any words. She cleared her throat and managed to say, "Goodnight Mr. Martin. I'll see you tomorrow."

Dave closed the door, but waited until he heard the lock turn before he headed back to his truck humming an unknown song. Laura stood in the entryway, taking off her coat and hung it in the front closet. Newt greeted her by rubbing up against her leg. She picked up the cat and petted him while she retired to her room. She spoke softly to her furry companion, "Maybe I'm not too old for this."

***

In a dark dingy bar down in the 'barrio' of Santa Ana, Sean had been drinking whiskey shooters most of the night. The locals left him alone figuring him to be lost, crazy, or a cop. Mariachi music and laughter filled the bar. There were old tired men sitting around telling stories, wasting their time until they had no choice, but to go home. One old drunk came up to Sean speaking in broken English.

"Hey gringo, I tink you miss your exit to red neck bar. You better go home be wid your own kind before some cholo tinks you easy money."

Sean turned to the old drunk. He tried his best to come across warm and friendly. "Thanks old man, I'll keep that in mind."

The old man stumbled and nearly fell over a bar stool. "De nada." Two young women, seated at a table nearby, giggled at the old man's folly. After the old man gained control of his near fall and returned to his seat, the younger of the two women left her table. Her black hair was weaved with different shades of bleached blonde. Her plump body was bulging out of black spandex pants and a crop top. Her makeup was too much black eyeliner, mascara, and red black lipstick with a very pale foundation. She boldly placed herself on a stool next to Sean.

"You a cop, or are you just a stupid white boy?"

Sean had been waiting all night for one of the local women to proposition him. "Just a stupid white boy looking for some peace n' quiet."

She leaned over towards Sean making sure she was revealing the cleavage of her breasts. "Peace n' quiet? Not in this part of town for you gringo, you could find trouble like the old man say. Maybe, you looking for something sweet like dulce. You know what I mean?"

Sean removed a fifty-dollar bill and a piece of paper with some writing on it from his jacket pocket. He placed it on the bar so the woman could plainly see it. Then he picked up the money and returned it in his jacket pocket.

"Oh, I know what you mean, but all I need from you is to talk into that telephone over there. You say what is on that piece of paper, but say it in Spanish and you can have that fifty and I'll leave."

She glared at Sean suspiciously. "I think you loco and you bring me trouble." Sean downed his shot glass of whiskey and slammed the glass down on the bar. He acted as thought he was preparing to leave.

"Fine. If you don't want easy money...."

The young woman interrupted his attempt to leave, in fear of missing the opportunity of making a quick buck.

"I didn't say I wouldn't. Give me that paper."

Sean was content his little ploy worked, slid the paper over to her.

"You can read English, yes?"

She snapped the paper out from under his hand. "Yeah, I read English."

While looking over the writing on the paper, she asked the bartender for a pen to re-write the words in Spanish above what was typewritten on the paper. She mumbled the Spanish verse over and over again. Sean was very pleased with the way things were working out.

"Good, you practice and make it sound real natural and when you're ready, I'll make the call, you talk, and I give you the money. Easy enough?"

She studied the paper some more. "Yeah, yeah... I have men ask for strange things, but nothing like this." She rehearsed her lines a few more times before she decided she was ready. "Okay let's do it."

She picked up the paper and headed for the pay phone, but Sean stopped her. "There is one more thing I need you to do."

The young woman retorted, "There's always one more thing with guys like you."

Sean tried to reassure her and spoke to her in a calm voice, "It's nothing kinky. I just want you to speak in a very soft, small voice. I want you to say this as though you mean it. Do you understand?"

She shrugged her shoulders. "Sure it's your money. I say it any way you want, gringo."

Together at the pay phone, Sean removed a $20 phone card from his wallet and another piece of paper, which had a long phone number on it. He dialed the number then entered the code from the phone card. The phone rang four times and an answering machine picked up. Satisfied he dialed the number to the warehouse in Juarez, he handed the receiver to the woman. She held the phone between her ear and shoulder, holding the piece of paper up so the faint hall light shone on it then proceeded to say the words in Spanish.

"Sr. Alvarez, ésta es Marie. Entiendo que mis padres me están pidiendo. Por favor dígales que no tengo ninguna intención de volver a México. Tengo trabajo y estoy en la escuela. Soy restante en América para hacerme una ciudadana. No cuidaron de mi cuando estaba allí, y me pidieron que para irse. Así pues, ahora éste es mi nuevo hogar. Por lo que me concierne ellos ya no tienen una hija, y yo no tengo padres. Así pues, por favor dígales que paren de buscarme. Déjenme sola, yo tengo una vida mucho mejor aquí. Gracias y adiós."

The woman hung up the phone pleased with her performance. She then held out her hand for her payment. Sean appeared to comply with her demand by taking the fifty out of his pocket, but then he held it back waiting for her to hand over the note in exchange for the money.

She reluctantly complied. Sean tore the piece of paper into as many pieces possible then placed them in his jacket pocket. He thanked the woman for a job well done.

Once he was on the freeway heading towards Rubidoux, he removed the torn paper from his pocket and let it blow from his hand out the window. He was content he had successfully completed his mission.

∗∗∗

At the Daniel's house, the alarm sounded off at seven A.M. Laura hit the snoozer and rolled over. Suddenly, she realized she only had two hours before Dave was to arrive. She quickly dressed in her sweats then proceeded out the door for her morning power walk. She was pleased she would have more than enough time to put in a good hour walk, and then shower, change and fix her face. She stepped up her pace to get the most out of her time.

Several miles away at the Martin house, Dave has already showered, shaved, and poured his morning cup of coffee, black. He glanced up at the clock and noted it was only seven-thirty. He tapped his fingers on the table, downed the rest of his coffee, and decided it was time to leave. Dave attached a note to the refrigerator with a banana magnet. It read:

Hey Girls,

Went to do a side job. Be back later.

If you need me, you have my number.

Love Dad.

The early morning drive was almost spiritual. The sun was filtering through the trees giving sharp contrast between the shadows and the sun lit sides of the trees and houses. The sky had not a cloud in it. It was such a color of turquoise if you were to paint a picture of it, you would say, "That can't be real, no sky is ever that blue." The air felt crisp, and the music sounded almost surreal as it came through the speakers. He could hear every distinct instrument and note it made. It was a good day; it was about to get better. For the first time in a very long time, there was a special woman in his life who was not related to him. He pulled up in front of the mobile home, checked the time on the dashboard clock. It was only eight-ten. Smiling to himself, he turned off the engine. Since he was almost an hour early, he decided to just sit back and bask in the morning sun.

Laura came around the corner and saw Dave's truck park in front of her home. A sense of panic hit her. "Ah man, he's got to be almost an hour early. I did say nine, didn't I? Oh my god, I don't have any makeup on. My hair is all sweaty. Oh yeah, these sweats are too sexy for words," she whined to herself. Deciding she could not run and hide she marched up to his truck. Dave was leaning back with his eyes closed looking very peaceful, very serene, and very handsome. She hesitated for a moment, and then tapped on the window. Startled, Dave sat up to see Laura waving at him.

"I'm sorry. I didn't mean to startle you. Yes I did, and you deserve it." She said with an impish smile on her face.

As he opened the door to exit, he questioned, "Deserve it? How so?"

"A gentleman never ever, never ever, ever, arrives before the woman has had a chance to make herself look presentable, that's why. You have girls you should know that."

Laura removed her wrist bracelet with the house key. She then unlocked the front door as Dave watched her over the hood of his truck.

"You look fine. You're one of those women who looks good with or without makeup. Just like my girls you worry about it too much."

Laura opened the door and glanced back at Dave with a look of disbelief. "Well, you might as well get what you need and bring it in. I'll show you where the problem is," she said while giving him a look that had a slight growl to it.

Dave rushed to retrieve his tools from the truck and followed Laura inside where she pointed out the line of dead outlets and then Matt's room.

"The fuse box is in here. Matt is at work so we'll have to move his mess to the side of the room so you can get to it. Matt and I checked the fuses and they all seemed to be okay. It was just after that I was stumped."

Dave peered into Matt's room. "I see your kids aren't any better at keeping their rooms clean than mine. Where is the main line into the house?"

"I think it's behind the shed. That's where all the meters are. Do you want me to show you?"

Dave placed his toolbox down on the breakfast counter and opened it. He removed some sort of battery-operated gadget which determined live and dead lines.

"Nah, I'll be able to find it. You go take care of what ever it is you need to do and I'll just go about my business fixn' as I go. All right, pretty lady?"

Laura removed her hair clip then shook the sweaty hair at the nape of her neck with her hand.

"I'll shower, change and be out momentarily." She said still feigning some annoyance.

While in the shower, Laura felt uncomfortable with a strange man in the house. She felt very exposed and vulnerable. She quickly dressed in the bathroom as though she could be seen through the door. As soon as she was properly covered, she opened the door to let the steam escape so she could use the hair dryer. Dave was nowhere in sight. She put a modicum of makeup on then headed straight into the kitchen to make coffee. She ground some beans and placed them in the filter, added water to the well, and then turned on the pot. The red indicator light went on, and then immediately turned off. Dave entered through the side door moments later.

"I just turned the power off. Hope you weren't in the middle of anything? I think I found the problem. It looks like you have a few dead wall sockets. The box in Matt's room will ultimately need to be replaced, but for right now I can replace some of the major fuses. You also have a secondary fuse box in the closet in your room, which will need fuses. I highly recommend you have this entire place rewired. It's really old not to mention aluminum."

"That sounds serious and expensive."

"Serious yes, because we don't want this place to burn down around you. Expensive, most of the expense is labor and you have me. As for today, I'll take care of the fuses and the dead wall sockets and anything else I find that I can take care of with what I have with me. It'll only take me a minute to replace it, and voila you'll have light."

Dave wandered into the front room and moved a wood chest away from the wall to change out one of the dead sockets. Laura followed behind him. "And a coffee maker, hair dryer, garbage disposal, and hopefully an oven again."

Dave positioned himself on the floor then proceeded to remove the old socket. All of a sudden, there was a strange and unfamiliar noise behind him. Dave jumped at the sound and swung around. "What the heck was that?"

Laura strolled over to the wooden room divider and retrieved Newt from the top by his harness. "Just the cat showing off his macho maleness. You had better watch out. He's a pretty curious beast. I wouldn't be a bit surprised if he climbed up on your head to see what you're doing."

Dave grinned, "Sounded more like a small earthquake."

Laura fetched the cat down and locked him in her bedroom. As she returned, she remarked, "I think we are better off if I keep him locked in my room. He'll attack just about anything, doesn't matter if it's moving, or not."

"Some guys get all the breaks." Dave said as he examined a new wall socket and straightened out the wires.

Laura blushed, "Keep your mind on your work. You do that just to see if you can get a reaction from me, don't you?"

Dave squinted as he peered up where Laura was standing. "Yep," he said as he returned to finish preparing the socket. Out of the corner of his eye, he noticed a drawing board in the corner of the room. There was a painting on the board, but was covered. "Who's the painter?" He queried.

Laura hesitantly went over to the drawing table and proceeded to wipe away the dust. "I am. It's a hobby, keeps me busy when the boys are gone." She said slightly embarrassed at how dusty her home had become.

Dave picked up the corner of the towel covering the drawing. "May I see your work?"

Laura was proud of her work, but at the same time sensitive about people's perception of it. Her need to be affirmed took precedence. "Sure." Laura removed the cloth to expose a watercolor painting of a baby in blue coveralls lying on a floor crying at the viewer. Dave remained silent as he examined the details of the picture. Impressed by her work he asked, "This is good. Do you have more?"

"Oh yeah, I have a lot more. They are all in a folder packed away in the closet."

"May I see them?"

Laura took a large cardboard folder out of the front closet. She placed it on the dinning room table, caring for its contents as one would a Stradivarius.

"This is the sum total of all my work for the past I don't know, twenty, thirty years. You can see the development. I wasn't very good at first, but now that the boys are older I can spend more time developing my eye hand coordination not to mention creative style." Laura turned each painting over for Dave to view. "They are pretty much in chronological order." When she came to a painting of a young boy coming down a park slide, she remarked, "This one was one of the first water colors I did. I really like the way it turned out. So, I've stuck with the water colors ever since."

Dave was impressed yet a bit surprised. "You are an incredibly talented woman. Who's this picture of?"

"Thank you. They are all taken from snap shots I've collected over the years of my kids, my parents, and me. The boy on the slide is Matt."

The next picture was of a young woman clad in a two-piece bathing suit standing in the surf of the ocean.

"That's of my mom. She was a beautiful woman don't you think?"

The painting was of this beautiful woman; it almost had the appearance of being a photograph. Dave held the picture up, comparing the painting with Laura.

"Yes she was. You sure can tell you are your mother's daughter. I have a question. Why do you have these boxed up and hidden away? Why aren't they hanging all over your walls, or in galleries?"

"That's real simple. It's a matter of money. It is not cheap to mat and frame just one of these. On my budget that would be a frivolity I cannot afford. The best I can do is photograph them and put them up on my web site."

Dave placed the painting down with immense care and then with equal care turned over the next one. "So, you have a web site. Hm, so there is some good stuff on the World Wide Web. Maybe someday you'll be a famous artist," he mused.

Laura had always hoped she could make a name for herself, but with thousands of starving artists competing for the same spot, her chances were slim to none. "I doubt it, not in this lifetime. Most of them had to be dead first before they were recognized, or appreciated. I just do it because I enjoy it," she said in truth.

Laura packed up the paintings and returned them back to their place in the closet.

Dave meandered back over to the painting still uncovered on the drawing board. "There has to be something more you can do to display this talent. This shouldn't be hidden away." His voice rang with resolve.

Laura replaced cloth over the painting with the similar care. She sighed, "In God's time."

"Well I think God and I are going to have a little discussion about speeding up that time line."

"I think that's going to be a one sided argument, and you're going to lose. Now, how about completing that work, so I can finally have my morning coffee? I'm having caffeine withdrawals. Anyway, I have to show you how to use that thing called a spoon."

The task completed Dave flipped the main switch back on. They tested all the known dead lines. Content the job was done they settled down outside on the patio for coffee and croissants. The morning air had warmed up, and once in a while a soft breeze blew the wind chimes while they sat at the table talking. Laura had brought Newt out and placed him on a leash. Dave reclined on one chair with his feet resting on another. He pet the cat, which had jumped up on his lap.

"I have never seen a cat with a harness much less a leash. How in the world did you ever get him to cooperate?"

Laura untangled Newt's leash as she spoke, "The first time I was successful placing the harness on him, I had to wait 'til he was sound to sleep. He still does not like to be walked, or should I say dragged, but he will tolerate being tied up out here while I'm outside with him. I've also tried to toilet train him, but that's not going too well."

Dave lifted Newt up, looking him square in the eyes. "Yeah we men do tend to tolerate strange demands from our women, don't we?" He said to the cat dangling from his hands then put the cat back down on his lap. "Have you ever thought about teaching people to draw and paint, to be their mentor so to speak?"

Feeling a little nervous Laura kept busy by refilling their cups with fresh coffee. "I've thought about it. I don't know if I'm qualified to teach, or even have a clue as how to teach people what I've just kind of figured out how to do. Why do you ask?"

"Trisha has always loved to draw; she just hasn't developed it. I think if she saw your work she would jump at the chance to learn."

"So there is a price to your charity. Now it's pay back time. Huh?"

"No, no, no, it's not that…it's... well if it keeps you around me more, then all right, yeah, it's pay back time." He grinned.

"Maybe something could be worked out, but only if Trisha is really interested. Okay?"

Dave leaned back with his feet back up on the other chair, grinning like a Cheshire cat. "Deal."

Laura decided it was time to ask him a question, which had been gnawing at her since the day she met him. "How come out of all those women that night you decide on me?" She quizzed.

"The kind of woman I have looked for is not only the kind you bring home to meet Mom and Dad, but the kind you are comfortable to be around and proud to introduce to your children. The kind of woman when you wake up next to the morning after doesn't scare the bee-gee-bees out of you. The last part maybe a guy thing or maybe it's just a Dave thing. I'm not sure… I could tell the first time I saw you, you were that woman." Dave responded without hesitation.

Laura paused for a moment. "I'm not sure I know how to respond to that."

"Then don't. No response necessary."

They sat in silence for a moment while the wind chimes sang a little song. Dave finished off the last of the croissants.

"Tell me, how long have you been a country western fan?" Dave asked.

"I'm not, I like it okay, and some of the music is really nice, but I don't think I've bought two CDs in the last five years that were country."

"Then what's with all the CDs by the computer? From what I could tell they were all country."

"Those are all Matt's. If you had looked over by the other computer you would have seen nothing, but Death Metal; I think they call it that. Those aren't mine either."

"Then what kind of music do you like?"

Laura tapped her fingers on the table. "I am particularly fond of jazz and rhythm'n blues." She said.

"Other wise known as elevator music." Dave poked fun at her.

"As I have always said, the day I am stuck between floors in an elevator with the man of my dreams is the day that music becomes elevator music." Laura calmly stated.

This time Dave was at the disadvantage. He lowered his head for a moment then exhaled. "Now I don't know what to say."

Laura grinned; she liked that fact that she took him off guard. She poured the last of the coffee into Dave's cup. The sound of Matt's VW could be heard as it rounded the corner. He pulled up in front of the house, parking behind the truck. Both Matt and Kyle traipsed up the stairs. Matt was still in his work clothes, and Kyle was dressed in his usual garb, this being a T-shirt with pictures from some album cover which bordered on the edge of obscene, or just grotesque, a pair of black vinyl pants with numerous buckles and chains, spiked bracelets, black lipstick, nail polish, and black Army boots. Matt approached Dave, extending his hand, and introduced himself then his brother. Kyle nodded his head acknowledging Dave, and barely audible said, "Nice to meet you." Laura's heart sank. There was no way she was ready to have Dave meet Kyle. Over the past year, she had difficulty herself adjusting to seeing her son's new demeanor. In Laura's mind, this was it; the man was going to bolt. She calmly looked up at Kyle and noticed a downhearted face.

"You're home a day early; what's the matter?"

Kyle raised his eyes. His voice was almost inaudible. "Megan and I had a fight. We broke up."

Laura took his hand, which he retracted. "I'm so sorry, hon. If you want to talk; you know I'm here for you. I know it's Mom you'd be talking to, and it's hard to talk to Moms, but…I love you. You know that don't you?"

Kyle continued to stare at the ground. "Yeah, I know that. I'm going inside." He disappeared inside the house, and Matt plopped in a seat at the table outside with Dave and Laura. No sooner, did he sit down; he picked up the carafe and shook it.

"Hey Mom, do you have any more coffee and some food? I'm starving."

Laura retrieved the carafe and the empty plates. "I'll go make some more and bring you guys some sandwiches."

From the kitchen window, she could see Matt and Dave talking up a storm like they were old buddies. After she made sandwiches, she brought a plate to Kyle's room, knocked on the door and entered. His room was dark except for the lights coming from his stereo. He removed the headset so he could respond to his mother's offer. "Thanks, but I'm not hungry."

Laura set the plate on the nightstand determined to make sure he would not go hungry. "Just in case you change your mind."

Closing the door behind her, she returned to the kitchen to retrieve the plate of sandwiches, napkins, a coffee cup, and a new pot of coffee. Upon seeing her move towards the door, Matt jumped up to open the sliding glass door so she could bring them their food.

"That looks great Mom. Dave here was telling me they might have an opening at the job site for general laborers. I wish I could take it, but he doesn't think they would work around my school schedule. Maybe next semester I could take night classes and work days. It certainly sounds better than what I'm doing now. Anyway he said they'd probably hire Kyle."

Dave started to take a bite of his sandwich, but stopped to clarify. "He couldn't wear the lipstick and the nail polish though. I don't think that would go over too well with the guys." He finished the sentence with a wink.

Laura wiped some debris off the table more to fidget than to clean. "That would be wonderful. He needs something to keep him busy, but I'm not sure he'd take the job." Her hands slightly shook as she swept the crumbs from the table as she spoke.

A flash of anger crossed Matt's face, as he adjusted himself in his chair. "Well, you could make it an either or situation for him Mom. He doesn't do anything around here except sleep, talk on the phone, play on the computer, or watch TV." Matt snapped.

Laura did all she could to keep her voice and mannerisms calm. Yet, she needed to let her son know he had had his say and the conversation was now over.

"Not today Matt, not today."

Matt was determined not to let it drop. "I'm not saying today," he said in his defense.

"The offer is open, Laura. There's no big rush. Anyway, I'm not sure there is a job opening. It's all up in the air for now. I'll know better in a couple of days." Dave interrupted trying to be diplomatic.

There was a look of sadness, or perhaps defeat in Laura's eyes. "Thanks."

Matt finished the last sandwich and brushed the crumbs from his lap. "Well folks I must excuse myself. I need a shower and a shave. Sara and I are having our own pre-Christmas exchange tonight. It was real nice meeting you, Dave. I'm sure we will be seeing a lot more of you around here." Matt said as he stood and extended his hand to Dave.

Dave reached up to shake Matt's hand. "If the lady will have me here, you bet."

Matt disappeared inside, and Dave could tell Laura's mood has turned sullen. "Kyle really troubles you, doesn't he?"

Laura sighed deeply. She so longed for the days when life seemed so much simpler. "Boy, is that an understatement. I also figured once you met him you'd be in your truck making tracks as far away from here as you could. I don't know what to do with him. I see two sides to him. One side is quiet, unassuming, shy, loving, and an extremely talented and intelligent young man. Then there's that facade of decadence and …and what. I don't even know what it is."

Dave reached over and placed his hand over Laura's. "This may sound crazy, but he reminds me of myself at that age. No really, the rebel without a cause. I still don't know what possessed me to enlist. Well, actually I do. My drinking buddy and I went down after a binge and signed up. It was our way out. Kyle just hasn't come to the conclusion that his life style doesn't work yet," Dave said in an attempt to comfort Laura. Then he knew he had to ask the crucial question. "Is he drinking and using?"

Laura looked hard into Dave's eyes. "I don't think so. If he is, he hides it real well because I have torn his room apart looking for anything illicit. His eyes always look normal, and I've not noticed any stoned behavior. I hope I'm not one of those mothers who just refuses to see it, but I've not seen anything to indicate that he's using. Then again I don't know what he is doing when he's not here."

Dave still holding her hand attempted to reassure her. "That's good. There's hope for him. Look at me. If God can straighten my sorry ass out, then there's hope for Kyle."

Laura smiled as she shook her head. "I find it hard to believe you were ever any other way than what I see today."

"Let me put it to you this way. Most of the people I hung with are either still drunks or dead, mostly dead. I was one of the lucky ones. I got clean and sober early and with the help of AA was able to stay that way."

"AA, do you still go?"

"Occasionally, every once in a while I need a reminder of where I came from so I know what not to go back to."

Matt exited out the sliding glass door with a bag full of gifts to give his mom a kiss before leaving. "I should be back around ten. I can't wait to see Sara's face when she sees what I got her." He turned and extended his hand again to Dave. "I'll see you later Dave. You take good care of my mom, you hear."

Dave being a gentleman stood and shook his hand. "I will always do my best, young man."

With his packages in hand, Matt gave his mom a kiss on the cheek and took off. Dave watched as the Bug bounced over a speed bump. He turned to Laura and asked, "He's not presenting this girl with a ring, or something like that is he?"

"Oh Lord no. She collects those beanie-babies, and he thinks he found every one she didn't already have. They are just friends, buddies. He has always had a lot of female friends."

"That's good cuz' at his age the last thing he needs is a serious relationship."

"That sounds more like you're reminiscing."

"That transparent am I?"

"Sometimes."

"Speaking of Christmas, what did you get the boys?"

The older the boys grew to be, the harder it was for Laura to figure out what to buy them. It had gotten to where she dreaded Christmas.

"Computer upgrades and clothes." She said.

Computers he could understand, but clothes were another issue.

"How the heck do you buy for Kyle?"

There was no way Laura would buy Kyle the kind of clothes he would want to wear, so she purchased what she thought he needed.

"I got him interview clothes I thought he just might wear."

Dave understood this considering what he had just seen. "Good move. Clothes always work for my girls."

A beeping sound could be heard from Dave's truck. He attended to its beckoning.

"I'll be right back. I guess one of my girls must be paging me."

He was gone for a few minutes. When he came back, his face was difficult to read. Dave was trying very hard to be diplomatic.

"Trish needs a ride. I really don't want to leave, but duty calls. Laura can I have your phone number? I really feel awkward just showing up here."

Laura spoke in her own flirtatious way, "Actually, I've rather enjoyed it, but yes you can have my phone number. Here let me write it down for you." She scribbled the number down on a piece of paper and handed it to Dave. "Good luck getting through." She added.

Dave took the piece of paper, folding it and placing it in his wallet, which he returned to his back pant pocket. "I'm persistent if nothing else."

"I can see that."

She followed Dave to his truck. He placed the toolbox on the floor of the truck, the passenger side and shut the door. Looking at the ground deep in thought, he paused to say what he thought might be his only chance to tell her what was on his heart.

"Laura, I.... I want you to know I am growing very, very fond of you, and I want to spend as much time as possible getting to know all there is to know about you. I know this is all happening really fast, and I don't want to scare you away. It's just that it's not often someone as special as you comes into this man's life. Life passes by so fast, and I don't want to look back with regrets. I guess what I'm trying to say is... is I'd like you to be a part of my life, a very special part of my life."

Laura was taken off guard by his candor, but in her heart she had hoped he wanted to be that special someone in her life.

"When you say it like that how could this woman refuse?"

Dave cupped Laura's face with both his hands. "Anyway you have art lessons to give to my daughter." He slowly brought his mouth to hers. This kiss had passion, this kiss had fire works, and this kiss was the start of a most wondrous romance.

"Merry Christmas, pretty lady. I'll call you later."

***

During the next few months, Dave and Laura grew closer. Kyle begrudgingly took the job at the construction site. Of course, he was not given much of a choice in the matter. Matt was showing an interest in

Alicen and she back, which made both Dave and Laura feel more than a little awkward. Trisha was enjoying her newfound artistic abilities and decided she wanted to go to school to be an art teacher. Life was good. Life was very good.

When Valentine's Day came, Dave had planned a surprise night out with the help of the kids from both sides. Josh had also been enlisted in his elaborate plans. Laura, on the other hand, had struggled with what to give Dave. Nothing seemed appropriate. No store bought card said the words she felt in her heart, so she sat down at her drawing table to produce her own. She tried to keep it simple; the first draft said, "If my heart had wings…It would fly straight to you." The second said, "My searching heart… Stood still the day I first saw you." The third, "My heart of hearts… Sings day and night, love songs just for you." All ended up crumpled in the trash. Frustrated, Laura sat staring at a blank piece of paper on the drawing board. Coaxing herself, she said, "From the heart Laura, write from your heart." Elbows on the drawing table, her head placed in the palm of her hands she stared blankly at the paper. A few moments passed by then the words began to flow onto the paper. Taking the rough draft, she placed it aside then removed a new piece of paper from a drawer and folded it in half. Having drawn a half moon with stars, she removed her brushes and the watercolors out of their case. She applied a light wash of blue around a drawing of a crescent moon and stars. On the outside, she wrote, "If Dreams and Wishes Were to Come True." Taking a calligraphy pen, she rewrote her poem inside. Once done, she waved the card in the air to help the ink to dry and then placed it in an envelope. "Now all I have to do it get up the courage to give this to him."

Laura glanced over at the wall clock. "Oh shoot, I'm going to be late." Dave had told her he needed a ride home from Josh's because his truck broke down and it was in the shop. As fast as she could, she dressed up in a new pair of slacks and sweater. She grabbed the card, purse, keys, and made her way out the door.

As she pulled up in front of Josh's house, she could see a limousine parked out front. She parked the car out on the street and then hesitantly hiked towards the house. A man stepped out of the limo, holding a large white box with a single red rose with a sprig of baby's breath. "Ma'am this is for you." The driver placed the box in her arms then he handed her a card. Trying to balance the box in one arm, she fumbled with the card in the other. It said, "Something pretty for a pretty lady. Next clue is at the front door. Dave." Looking up at the front door of Josh's house, she noticed another red rose with a note attached to it. As she took the rose with the card down from the door, the card fell to the ground. Kneeling down trying not to drop the box, Laura opened the second note. It simply read, "Open door." She obediently opened the door to find Dave standing there in a black tuxedo holding yet another red rose. "Surprise!" he said as he walked up to her, handing her the rose, then gave her a kiss on the cheek. "I think you need to go in that room right there and change your clothes."

Laura dumbfounded looked around. "What's going on? Where's Josh and Joyce? Why are you all dressed up?" She asked.

Dave grinned mischievously as he gently placed his finger to her mouth. "Shh … Nobody's here. You need to change cuz we are going out. Now go on, go." He pointed her in the direction of Justin's old bedroom. In the room, Laura placed the box on the bed and untied its red bow. There she found everything she could possibly need for her night out on the town. The box contained a beautiful off white semiformal dress, nylons, shoes, earrings, and an ornate hair clip.

Once dressed, she took the ornate hair clip, wrapped her hair to the back, and placed the clip in her hair. She returned to the living room where Dave was seated reading a newspaper, enjoying one of Josh's cigars. Upon seeing her enter the room, he put the paper down and the cigar out.

"You get more beautiful every day."

Laura twirled around displaying her new dress. She asked, "Everything fits perfectly. How did you know?"

Dave was pleased everything was turning out so well. He picked up a shawl and placed it around her shoulders. "I had a little help from some young people we both know. Shall we go? The car is waiting." He replied with his usual wink.

Laura snatched up her three red roses and gave him a quick kiss on the cheek. "You're going to have a real hard time topping this one."

After almost an hour's ride, the car finally pulled up to Delaney's in Newport Beach. They sat at a table over looking the ocean inlet. Before dinner arrived, Laura pulled out the homemade card.

"This seems so small compared to this evening you're giving me, but I'd like you to have this."

She handed him the card and watched him as he opened it and read her poem. She anxiously waited while he read her card looking for a sign if he was pleased with her small, but heartfelt gift.

The words of her poem greeted his eyes and warmed his heart. It read:

If dreams and wishes were to come true
I'd dream of a man just like you
I would wish upon stars every night
To make our days shiny & bright,
Like the sun glistening on the open sea
That is what my wishes and dreams would be.
To live a life in the arms of the man I love
Blessed by God and the angels above.
We would stand together against the winds of
time
Knowing our love was the ultimate find.
If dreams and wishes were to come true
I'd dream dreams of only you."

Dave sat there for the longest time reading the card over. Then he reached across the table and took hold of her hand.

"You wrote this?" Laura nervously shook her head yes. Dave continued, "This is the most beautiful gift I have ever received. You're going to have a hard time topping this one."

He brought her hand to his mouth and kissed it and Laura breathed a sigh of relief.

After dinner, they walked on the beach hand in hand. It was a perfect evening. He was her perfect man and she his perfect woman.

The Discovery

The city of Mayville is located at the western end of Chautauqua Lake in upstate New York. It is a small metropolitan area with farming communities as part of it borders. The area is known for its lush rolling green hills, beautiful trees, and the lake for its fishing, boating, and recreation. Like all small communities, life moves at a slower pace.

The long winter had ended, and the snow had completely melted. The ground had thawed enough to start the spring garden. Erik had gassed up the rotary tiller. He started it up, it sputtered, and died. He placed his foot against the engine and pulled the cord a couple more times to finally hear it purr. Adjusting the gears, he set it to the hard ground. The tiller ripped through the ground with ease. Kay rolled the wheelbarrow to the edge where the ground had just been tilled. She picked up rocks and placed them in the wheelbarrow.

Nearby, Nathan and Julie were running around trying to get their kite to fly. "Come on Nathan. You're not running fast enough," Julie said as she held the kite tight in her little hands. She waited for a gust of wind then let go. Nathan took off running as fast as he could. This time the kite caught the wind, and it flew high up into the sky. Julie clapped her hands, giggling with excitement. Kay smiled as the children played.

There had been another strike with the autoworkers union, and car production had been drastically reduced. Therefore, there was no need for the steel, and Erik had been laid off at the foundry. They could not continue to afford the house payments, and it went into foreclosure. It had been most fortunate that the old farmhouse became vacant. The Sheltons, long time friends, offered their old home to them until they could get back on their feet. No one thought the strike would go this long. Erik could not wait any longer for the strike to be over, so he did odd jobs in and around town during the week. Weekends he worked at the car wash for minimum wage. Foundry work was nothing to brag about, but working at the car wash crushed his spirit. He felt so inadequate as a husband, father, and provider. His mood was surly most of the time. The only thing he had been looking forward to was the spring planting. The garden took his mind off his troubles.

Erik pushed the tiller with a mission. Suddenly, the tiller hit something hard. He thought it might be a large stone, or a tree root which would have to be dug out. He shut down the tiller and placed his shovel in the dirt to dig out the obstruction. As he pulled the shovel out with its load of dirt, he saw something odd protruding from it. He set the shovel down and brushed the dirt away from the object. Kneeling on the ground, he removed his handkerchief out of his back pocket then picked the object from the dirt. Horror, absolute horror filled his body as he realized he was looking at a partially decomposed hand.

Kay curious about what had captured Erik's attention, shouted over to him. "What you got there?"

Erik's face was ashen white. As quickly as he could, he assessed the situation, determining what his next line of action should be.

"Kay, I want you to take the kids in the house and call the police."

This statement caught Kay's attention. She started to walk over to where Erik was squatting. He raised one hand to signal her to stop. "Kay, I said I want you to take the kids in the house and call the police, NOW." He ordered.

The look on his face frightened her. She could feel her heart racing, and her mind filled with a hundred questions. "And what do you want me to tell the police, Erik?"

Erik covered the hand with his handkerchief. He deliberately kept his voice calm as he explained to her what needed to be relayed to the police.

"You tell them I found what looks like a body in my garden. You tell them it doesn't look like it's been here very long. Okay? Can you tell them that?"

The dogs curious about all the commotion came over sniffing the ground where Erik had dug up the hand. He grabbed the dogs by their collars.

"I'll put the dogs in the pen. Now get going."

Kay ran over and rounded up the kids. They complained all the way, as she marched them into the house. She set them down in the living room and turned on the television. "Okay, you can have your TV time now." The children were left in the family room, while she charged for the phone.

In the kitchen-dinning room area, Kay removed the receiver from the wall set and dialed the number for the local police. A voice at the other end spewed out, "Chautauqua County Sheriff's Department, is this an emergency?" Kay stammered, "No, it's not an emergency, but it is important." She was immediately put on hold. Kay held the receiver so tight her knuckles started to turn white.

Nathan and Julie sat on the living room floor in front of the television periodically peering into the dinning room to see what mom was so panicky about. Finally, a voice came back on the line. "How can I help you ma'am?" Kay was trying to keep herself composed while she relayed the information to the voice on the other end. "I think you need to send someone up here right away."

The voice on the phone questioned, "And what seems to be the problem ma'am?" Kay took a deep breath, and then blurted out, "My husband was tilling the soil in our garden, and he found a body, a human body. A… a dead body."

Now loaded with this information the dispatcher preceded with her questionnaire. "Can I have your name ma'am?"

"Kay…Kay Andersen."

"And your address?"

"We live on Beaujean Road just past Crawford Road at the old Shelton farm house. Do you know where that is?"

There was a moment of silence while the dispatcher wrote down all the information. "Yes ma'am. We will have a car out there right away. Do you have the area where you found the body secure?"

"What...what do you mean?"

The dispatcher patiently explained, "Ma'am, it is very important the area where you found this body remains undisturbed. It is necessary to protect this area so we can collect evidence. Is this being done?"

Kay peered out the dinning room window curtains. There she could see Erik sitting on a not yet split log he had placed near the body. He was staring at the dirt where his handkerchief covered the exposed hand. The shovel was leaning against the wheelbarrow several feet away from him.

"Yes ma'am, my husband is out there now. We have the dogs penned up, and the kids are in the house. How soon can you have someone here?"

"They are on their way now." The dispatcher replied.

Almost as the words came out of her mouth, three squad cars tore up the gravel driveway. Sheriff Robert Ecklund of the Chautauqua County Task Force was first to arrive. The County Task Force was responsible for collecting evidence at a crime scene. It included members of the Jamestown Police Department, Chautauqua County Sheriff's Department, New York State Police, Town of Ellicott Police Department, the Federal Bureau of Investigation, Chautauqua County District Attorney's Office, and the Pennsylvania State Police. Sheriff Ecklund found Erik still seated on the log staring at the dirt. As Sheriff Ecklund walked towards him, Erik shouted out, "I thought it was a root or something. Never, never in my wildest dreams would I have ever thought it was this."

The dogs were nervously barking in their pen as Sheriff Ecklund approached the area of the covered hand. "You must be Mr. Andersen. I'm Sheriff Ecklund. Let's see what you've got here."

The officers from the other two squad cars were busily taking equipment needed for their investigation out of the trunk of their cars. Sheriff Ecklund knelt down and removed the handkerchief with a pen from his pocket. He examined the hand, moving the deformed looking digits. Then he leaned over to examine the hole left by the shovel to see part of a bone protruding from the dirt. "No, that's definitely not a root. Looks like you tore the hand up pretty good with the roto-tiller. The hand is missing the tips of its fingers."

Erik curiously looked down at the hand. "No, I don't think so. It looks to me like the tiller hit it at the forearm."

The sheriff reexamined the exposed body part and then at the hand. "You might be right."

Deputy Flanders arrived at the site with a brief case, four three-foot stakes, and yellow tape to quadrant off the area. Flanders took one look at the exposed hand and exclaimed, "It's a good thing the ground is still really cold. It sure has helped keep the body from decaying too badly. Otherwise, there would have been a good stink and those dogs of yours would have destroyed the evidence. Shall I go ahead and rope the area off, Sir?"

Sheriff Ecklund pondered on the proper procedures, "Go ahead Joe. Make sure you allow for about ten feet in any direction."

Deputy Flanders opened his briefcase, taking out a clipboard with graph paper already in place, a mechanical pencil, measuring tape, string, and a soil probe. Taking the soil probe, he examined the soil, which appeared slightly darker than the surrounding ground. Determining the approximate location of the body he proceeded to draw a map of the area called a 'plan view.' He constructed a perfect ten-foot square using a simple geometric formula. Once each point was established, he took flagged pins and pressed them into the ground.

The second deputy laden with camera, a portable argon laser, flashlight, and a large metal brief case arrived on the crime scene. Sheriff Ecklund stopped him. "I think outside of blocking the area off, pictures are all we are going to get today."

Deputy Paul Duncan set all of the equipment, except his camera, in the wheelbarrow. He proceeded to take pictures both with and without scale of the partially exposed body, the hand, and the surrounding area. Sheriff Ecklund continued, "When you're done here I want you to call Sgt. Frank Todora with the Jamestown PD. Ask him if he'll contact that Archeologist who worked on the Kathy Wilson case. We're going to have to set up just like an archeological recovery dig in order to get proper evidence. Also, put a call into the station. Confirm the find with Katie. Tell her to make the appropriate calls."

Flanders finished pounding the stakes into the ground then proceeded to attach the yellow tape to the poles. Deputy Duncan concluded his picture taking then politely asked, "Mr. Andersen, could I go inside and use your phone?" Duncan could have easily used the radio in his car or his cell phone but this was a perfect opportunity to have a look inside the house and talk to the wife, away from any influences of her husband.

Erik had been standing around feeling totally useless. "Yeah sure, the wife and kids are inside. Kay will show you in."

Erik could hear another car approaching the house. It slowed down and then turned into the driveway. Sheriff Ecklund shook his head when he realized who it was. "Mr. Andersen it appears the press has been monitoring the dispatch calls. The Post-Journal has some persistent reporters so if you don't want them on your property I'll have Flanders turn him away. Besides, I need to ask you a few questions. I can let Flanders give the standard PR."

Erik watched as a man in his late 40's with gray hair and an unlit cigar hanging out of his mouth approached them. The man had the appearance of a 'Colombo' like character. Erik had always kept to himself. The thought of having to talk to people, much less the press, was not on his social agenda. He knew he did not have the verbal skills or savvy to deal with the press. "It's going to be a circus around here for a while, isn't it?" He said with a wince in his voice.

A dead body found in this poor man's garden was big news for this little community. It was definitely more exciting than last week's news of Delahoy's cows escaping, and then ending up blocking traffic down the only main highway in town for three hours. Sheriff Ecklund understood Erik's dilemma. He shook his head. "Yep, I'm afraid so."

Erik could see two little faces staring out the dinning room window trying to understand the reason the police cars were parked outside. They suddenly disappeared and Kay pulled the shade down to block their view. He sighed, "Do whatever you have to do to keep those people away from my family. Kay and the kids are going to have enough to contend with. We sure don't need them hounding us too."

Sheriff Ecklund's eyes connected with Flanders. He tilted his head toward the oncoming reporter, and Flanders immediately headed off in his direction. He detained the reporter a good twenty-five yards away from where the body was discovered. They talked for a minute, but the reporter was obviously not happy with the lack of information he had been given. He tried to step around Deputy Flanders. Flanders moved to counter him. Then the reporter yelled out. "I just want to get an official statement from you, Sheriff."

Sheriff Ecklund turned to Erik and sarcastically spoke, "He just wants a picture of the dead body." Noting the forlorn look on Erik's face, he changed his tone. "Mr. Andersen, why don't you go inside? I'll take care of the press."

A sense of relief filled every fiber of Erik's being. He had been waiting for two hours for someone to either give him something to do, or dismiss him. Obediently, his body leaned toward the house. Erik shook his head yes with a sense of urgency. "I think that's a good idea, a damn good idea." As he headed toward the house, Sheriff Ecklund yelled out to him. "Would you tell Deputy Duncan to come out as soon as he is done with his calls?" Erik raised his hand to acknowledge him without turning around. "Sure thing, Sheriff." The reporter straight away turned to walk towards Erik, and Flanders detained him again.

"Mr. Andersen, could I ask you a few questions please?" the reporter yelled out.

Erik again raised his hand without turning around. "I have no comments," he said as he disappeared into the old house.

Sheriff Ecklund joined Flanders and the reporter without delay. It was important the ground rules were set. He greeted the reporter with curtness in his voice, "Hello Ron." These two words spoke volumes, and it was meant to. The tone in his voice said this was his territory, and Ron was to tread lightly.

Ron Ellis had been a reporter for the Post most his life. He had done some freelance work, but never received much recognition. This area of New York did not have much violent crime. Therefore, when it did, it was big news. Ron was always the first reporter on location of a breaking news story. He was known for his bulldog tactics, and age had not slowed him down one bit. He intentionally tried to smooth over his rough demeanor for the sheriff, hoping it would ingratiate him. It came across as a gruff whine.

"Sheriff Ecklund, all I want is some details on what you found here."

Ecklund bit the inside of his mouth staring right through Ellis. He was not buying Ron's little performance.

"Ron, I believe my Deputy here gave you all the information we can at this time. I'll give an official statement when there is more information to give."

Ron was not satisfied with this response either. He just did not like the idea of a public statement, for it meant he was not first with the information.

"Come on Bob. I'm getting too old for this. Can't you give me something the rest of the world won't get at the same time?"

A cool breeze kicked up. Sheriff Ecklund zipped up his jacket and placed his hands in his pockets. He was almost amused by Ron's groveling.

"Ron, you already have the lead on this story. That's all you're going to get for now. Mr. Andersen has requested you be removed from the property. If you refuse to go, I'll have to arrest you. Have I made myself perfectly clear?"

Ron removed the cigar out of his mouth. He spit loose tobacco he had bit off, onto the ground. The whine was gone now, and the old bulldog was back.

"You always play right from the rule book, don't you? Can't you ever cut anyone some slack?"

Ecklund had dealt with Ellis on two other occasions, neither one of them a pleasant experience. During the Wilson case, Ellis wrote pieces slanted towards police corruption and cover-up angle. He was not going to allow any of that nonsense this time.

"Ron, I'm going to give you two minutes to vacate the premises. If you aren't gone by then, I'll have my Deputy charge you with trespassing and obstruction of an impending investigation. **Now**, have I made myself perfectly clear?"

Ellis threw the cigar on the ground then took his right foot and stomped it into the dirt. "You've not heard the last of me, Sheriff. I'll get my story with or without you." He draped the strap of his camera over his shoulder and trekked back to his car. Sheriff Ecklund glared at the back of his head and to himself said, "I'm sure you will, Ron. I'm sure you will."

Deputy Duncan joined his commander and Flanders as Ellis was backing his car down the driveway. Duncan pulled out a note pad from the inside chest pocket of his jacket. He began to report the information he had obtained, but Ecklund interrupted him.

"How would you two like some easy, but boring overtime? I think it would be wise to have one of you stand watch over the site, just in case we have company of the four, *or* two-legged kind. The other can field calls for the Andersen's. I'm sure once the story goes to print they'll have more than just Ellis to contend with."

Both Deputies' agreed they would do the overtime duty. With that aspect taken care of, Ecklund was ready to hear what Duncan had to say. "Okay, Duncan what do you have for me?"

Duncan opened his note pad to make sure he did not miss any points and to get the names correct. "I called Sgt. Todora as you asked. He called me back just now and said the woman they used on the Wilson case was not available. So he contacted the State University of New York at Buffalo informing them what was going down and what we needed. They in turn contacted a Mashenka Vascovich, who is in their doctoral program of forensic anthropology. Vascovich will be here around noon tomorrow to set up the dig. The State Police and the FBI have been informed about the finding. As soon as we have more information available, the FBI will start running a missing person's report. The State Police said whatever we need, they are at our disposal. Is there anything else you needed, Sir? I'd like to go pick up a few things if I'm going to be here all night."

Ecklund pondered the information he had just been given then decided while Duncan was out he could take care of a few important tasks. "Yeah, there is one more thing. I want you to go up to the Shelton's. See who they have rented this house out to in the past year. What I'm hoping for is an application the renters would have submitted with references and emergency contacts. I'm certain the Andersens here are innocent of any wrongdoing. Oh yeah, while you're out, stop by Ivan's Grill. Pick up hamburgers, fries, and copious amounts of coffee.

Don't forget the cream and sugar this time." He pulled two twenties out of his wallet. "And I want my change back with a receipt."

Duncan enjoyed the investigative aspect of his job. If it also meant he had to be the gopher, then so be it. "I'll get right on it, Sir. I should be back in a few hours."

Sheriff Ecklund now turned his attention to the present situation. He instructed Flanders on his next job tasks.

"Flanders pick up that equipment from the wheel barrow and put it away. You get to stand guard over the dead while I play fifty questions with the Andresens"

Sheriff Duncan arrived at the station almost two hours later with a renter's application from the Sheltons in hand. The dispatcher was talking on the phone when he walked up to the front desk. It was apparent to Duncan it was a personal call: "Hey, Katie. Tell your boyfriend you will see him later. I've got some real important work for you to do."

Katie defensively corrected Duncan's perception, "It wasn't my boyfriend; it was my mother."

Duncan slapped his clipboard on the counter, feigning anger, "Yeah, yeah, whatever. You know you're not supposed to take personal calls while you're working, **but** you're such a cute little thing, I won't tell Ecklund, this time." He changed his tone in mid-stream purposely to keep Katie off balance.

Katie blushed, "Okay you've kissed up enough. Now what is it you want me to do?"

Katie was a pretty, but a very shy woman in her early twenties. The officers at the station loved to tease her just to see her blush. After three years with the department, she still had not been able to harden herself to their teasing. Duncan took two pieces of paper from his clipboard and handed them to her.

"First, I need a couple of photocopies of these. Then I need you to pull up names, addresses, and drivers' licenses that are on the application. I'm looking for records of convictions, traffic tickets, warrants, and alias's, anything you can come up with. Also, I've got a pretty good description of the guy who rented the Shelton house last summer. Call the FBI to see if they can come up with something. It still might be too vague, but we've got to start somewhere."

Katie dutifully took the papers, making several copies of each and placed the originals in a folder labeled Case #02-00034. She then took a copy for herself and handed the rest over to Duncan. She tried her best to give Duncan a hard time.

"I thought you got paid the big bucks for the investigative work."

Duncan was unfazed by her attempt to goad him and winked at her. "I do, but I'm up for a promotion. Supervisors are required to delegate. Besides, I know how much you love those murder mystery novels. This way you get to help uncover a real story."

Katie retrieved her copy of the renter's application from the counter. As she read it over, Duncan headed out the door to go buy burgers at Ivans down the street. She quickly scanned down the document, stopping at "In case of emergency contact." It read, Jack Richardson, Buffalo, New York. There was no address or phone number listed. She darted around the desk and ran out the front door to see Duncan pulling away. Katie waived the paper in the air at him as he started to pass her by. "Hey Duncan, Duncan," she screamed.

Duncan drove the car over to the curb, rolled down the passenger side window. He continued to tease her, "Missed me already did ya?"

Katie blushed, "Stop it, Duncan! I think I might have something for you."

Duncan was surprised yet skeptical. "Already?"

Katie proudly announced her discovery. "Yeah, I was looking over this application and it has this name here. Jack Richardson in Buffalo, New York. My sister was dating a Jack Richardson who worked for the narcotic's division with the Buffalo PD. He was a real work-alcoholic so she dumped him. I know it's a long shot, but what do we have to loose by contacting the guy. What do you think?"

Duncan's car radio squawked. It was Ecklund looking for his food. Duncan ignored his radio.

"Katie, I think you call the man, and while you're at it call Ecklund and tell him I went for the food. Ten-four?"

Katie held her hand out with a thumb up as Duncan drove off.

Mashenka Vascovich arrived at the Andersen house with her assistant Kevin Harris around eleven A.M. the next morning. The white van was meticulously packed with everything they would need for a long stay. Mashenka and her family had arrived in this country when she was around ten years old. Yet, she still had a distinguishable Polish accent. Her father had been one of the many who fought for Solidarity in Poland and subsequently was kicked out. She had been poor most of her life and had worked hard towards obtaining her doctorates. Vascovich was employed as a deputy with the Erie County (NY) Sheriff's Department scientific staff and as a private consultant in forensic anthropology. Kevin on the other hand came from a well-to-do family in Williamsville, a suburb north of Buffalo. He did not have the grades to attend an Ivy League College so he ended up at the University where he was doing his graduate studies. They worked well together as long as they did not discuss politics.

Deputy Hall had replaced Flanders early that morning. He had been briefed on Ms. Vascovich's arrival. He approached the van as they were taking the equipment out. "Ms. Vascovich, I'm Deputy Hall. If you follow me I'll show you where they found the body."

Mashenka pulled out the tent and poles. With her arms loaded, she addressed the Deputy, "Thank you, Deputy Hall." Then she spouted instructions to her associate, "Kevin, bring the rest of the camp setup over where the Deputy is taking me."

She followed the Deputy to the area where it had been taped off. Then she located a section of ground which was relatively flat and set the tent and the poles down where she decided they would set up camp. She walked over to the yellow tape square where she easily hiked her leg over. The hand was still covered with Erik's handkerchief. She uncovered the hand and examined it.

"Hmm…did you find the finger tips anywhere?"

Deputy Hall was puzzled by her question. "No ma'am. We didn't even look."

She probed the hole where the bone was protruding from the dirt. "You might want to bring up some tracking hounds, see if they can find them. It's not likely, but it might be worth a try."

The Deputy scratched his head. "Why do you say that?"

Mashenka still stooped on the ground, twisted around to look at the Deputy.

"Someone deliberately cut off the fingertips just at, or before the first knuckle so if discovered we couldn't get any fingerprints. I doubt very much if that same person left the evidence for us to find. It will be interesting to see what else was done to prevent our victim's identification."

Mashenka stood up and brushed her hands off on her old khaki jeans. She was a tall woman and towered over the Deputy by at least three to four inches. As Deputy Hall stared up at this Amazon like woman he remembered the paper Deputy Flanders asked him to give to her.

"Ms. Vascovich, I'll be right back. I need to get something the other officer left for you."

Kevin brought up the cots, portable tables, and sleeping bags. He placed them on the ground next to the tent and poles. This was his first field dig. He was brimming with excitement and curiosity. "Is it all right if I go take a look?"

Mashenka had already started unpacking the first tent. "Sure go ahead, but remember you'll be examining every inch of that body for probably the next year. It's going to become old and boring real fast." Kevin was undaunted by her words and jumped at the opportunity to get his first look.

Deputy Hall returned with the paper still set on the clipboard. "Ma'am, here it is. He called it a 'plan view,' thought you'd need it."

She studied the graph paper with great care. Looking it over, she compared the numbers and the drawing to the posts set in the ground.

She addressed to the Deputy, "You can tell the officer he did a damn good job. He set up the site almost perfect. This will come in handy not to mention save me a lot of time. Deputy Hall, that is your name correct?"

Hall responded, "Yes, ma'am."

She stooped down to touch the ground, checking its temperature. "I was thinking I'd like to keep the ground where the body is as cold as possible until we actually get to the point where we can extract it. This will delay any further decomposing. Could you arrange to get us a lot of dry ice?"

"I'll put a call in for it right now, plus I'll see about the tracking dogs." He said as he headed for his squad car.

Kevin satisfied with his first look rejoined Mashenka at the van to retrieve the rest of the equipment minus the generator.

"God, I sure hope those dogs settle down. It will be hard to concentrate with them barking like that."

"What dogs?" Mashenka said pan faced.

"What do you mean what dogs? Those dogs, the ones that have been going at it ever since we arrived."

"Oh, those dogs, I barely noticed." She said in a teasing tone. "They'll calm down once they get use to our scent. Come on. We have a lot of work to do. I'd like to actually start this dig today."

As Mashenka carried the next load of equipment up to the site, she saw two small faces staring out of a window back at her. She smiled at them and waved her hand as best she could from under her load. She thought to herself, "It's going to be a long few days for you guys if they keep you cooped up in there, but on the other hand I'm not sure I want you out here."

***

Detective Richardson arrived at the downtown precinct at around three o'clock. He was working the swing shift for the next few months. He was in his early forties and had been working narcotics for the past twelve years. Undercover work was usually left to the younger men, but since the baby boom, there were many addicts and dealers around his age. He was good at his job, good at recruiting informants particularly the female kind who had joined up with bad company. Jack did not mind the undercover look. Because of his work, he was allowed to keep his hair long and maintain a full beard. Not having to wear a uniform or a suit was also a big plus to him. Most everyone in the precinct probably would not even recognize him if he cleaned up. The down side was most women did not give him the time of day. He had dated a few female officers, but it never seemed to work out. Then because of his appearance, the type of civilian women who were attracted to him were less than desirable. He sat down at his desk and proceeded to filter through the mass of papers in his basket. Four or five items down he noticed a phone message attached to a fax. As he began to read the message, the phone rang.

"Detective Richardson.... Yes ma'am I did. As a matter a fact I have it in my hands right now…" He flipped the note back to expose the renter's application and read the information. "Can't say I know a John Talbert…or a Jorge Quinteros. No that name does not sound familiar either. I'm afraid they must be referring to a different Jack Richardson. I know of at least two others listed in the phone book. Maybe you should try contacting them. I'm sorry I couldn't be of more help.... Oh, you're Stacey's sister. How are you doing? Good. Good. And Stacey? Getting married. Well, good for her. Well, Katie if I think of anything that might help I'll be sure to give you a call."

Katie hung up the phone, disappointed her lead just went nowhere. She raised Deputy Duncan on the radio to inform him. He was back up at the Andersen place assisting fellow officers with the bloodhounds. The hounds had not picked up any scents in or around the house. They had taken them to the surrounding fields, then up into a small wooded area. It appeared Mashenka had been correct. No further evidence was going to be found.

Mashenka and Kevin started digging at the outer edges of the perimeter. A couple of students from the local college had been hired to sift through the dirt looking for any additional evidence. By the dirt coloration and soil probes, they had determined the body was buried in-tact at the center of the perimeter. Therefore, the first part of the dig would go rapidly until they came close to exposing the body. Mashenka had figured the body to be buried six to eight inches below the surface. They dug down a full twenty inches. By nightfall, they were within a foot of the body's estimated position. From here on, the work would proceed much more slowly. The shovels would be put away in favor of trowels, whiskbrooms, dustpans, and Perino picks. Mashenka looked up at the darkening sky.

"That's it for today, Kevin. Let's clean up and get something to eat."

The tracking dogs long gone, Deputy Duncan prepared to leave as the relief shift arrived. Mashenka had pulled the house garden hose over near the tents and clamped it to a stake to make a faucet to wash her hands when needed. The Deputy approached her as she splashed some water on her face.

"It looks like your getting close to exposing the body. I have the next two days off, but I'd like to come up to photograph the body. Could you call the station when the time comes?"

Mashenka wiped her face with a small hand towel. "Sure, but it's not necessary. I'll be taking pictures which the department will receive, as many copies as they may want, or need." She replied.

Duncan was a little intimidated by the intellectual type woman. He fidgeted with his keys. "Yes ma'am I know, my commander requested I also take pictures, for the experience, if you don't mind."

Mashenka rested the towel on the stake. It was not all that long ago she was in his shoes. "I'll call as soon as there is anything to photograph, and you can snap your little heart out."

Duncan tired from the day's search tipped his hat. "Thank you ma'am."

Mashenka shivered as the cool of the night settled in. As Duncan left, reporters and news crews located on the road at the base of the driveway attempted to obtain information from him to no avail.

The first day's work done she retired to her tent where Kevin had been heating up some soup and attempting to grill some cheese sandwiches on the Coleman stove. "Hi Hon, dinner's almost ready. Sorry about the burnt bread."

Mashenka sat on her cot and untied her boots. "You're really enjoying yourself here aren't you?"

Kevin handed her a large metal tin cup with soup and a paper plate with the well-done sandwich. "As a matter of fact I am. I find this all very exciting, don't you?"

Mashenka picked off some of the burnt crust off her sandwich and bit into it. "When I started out, I found I didn't work well with live witnesses. I couldn't deal with the contemptuous attitudes some people had, so I chose to work with the dead. They couldn't talk back, but they could give me a whole lot more information than the living were willing to give. The problem is I can't ever seem to forget that the body I am examining was once a real living human being, and right before they died they were terrorized and probably tortured. It is a very, very horrible way to die, and at times, it tears at my very soul. I get excited when I find some shred of physical evidence that will put the bastard in jail."

Kevin tilted his cup up then tapped it on the backside to make the final contents drop out into his mouth. The cup emptied, he placed it on the small table set up in her tent. "Anyone ever tell you that you internalize too much?"

"Yeah, my ex-boyfriend." She smiled a halfhearted smile. "So on that pleasant note I'm tired, I'm going to bed. See you in the morning."

Kevin removed the empty tin cups and the pans to wash them out. Before he secured the flap to her tent, he warmly said, "Goodnight Missy."

Mashenka unrolled her sleeping bag onto the cot, turned off the lantern, and snuggled in for a nights rest.

As the morning sun rose, the birds started to sing. The farmhouse, four tents, and the dig site were exposed to the dawn's rays. Mashenka, Kevin and the students each had their own tent. The fourth, contained equipment and a work area for examining the dirt excavated from the site. There was also a pine box to transport the body to more ideal working conditions at the University. The hope was today they would have the body fully exposed and removed.

Mashenka crawled out of her bag with only a large flannel shirt and socks on. She picked up the dirty pants, shaking them out before she pulled them on, and then tucked in the oversized shirt. As she pulled her boots on, Kevin shook the tent door. "Hey are you up and decent?"

Mashenka laced up her right boot. "Yeah, I'll be out in a minute."

Kevin stood outside admiring the landscape as the sun revealed the earth's beauty. "It sure is beautiful here. Take your time. Hey, I was talking to Mr. Andersen, and he said there's a small cafe down the road a ways that serves one hell of a breakfast. I thought I'd send the students down to pick us up something."

Mashenka departed the tent while she pulled a lined windbreaker over her head. "That sounds like a plan. That way we can get an earlier start. I want the body ready to be shipped out by tomorrow morning. The sooner we are done, the sooner these people can have some semblance of a life back."

As soon as her hands were free, Kevin handed her a cup of black coffee in a tin cup. "That's not likely. Not for a while yet. I understand their phone has been ringing off the hook since the story broke. Mr. Andersen has put a request in for a new unlisted number, but it may take a few weeks. The wheels grind mighty slow around here. Poor man, all he was trying to do was plant a vegetable garden; now he has this circus. He said something about trying to dig up the ground behind the house, not an ideal location, but it will keep him busy."

The coffee in Mashenka's cup turned cold. She poured the remainder on the ground and set the cup inside the tent. "The kids have to be driving him crazy. Well, come on let's see what we can get done before breakfast gets here."

It was around one thirty in the afternoon when they had most of the dirt removed from the top and sides of the body. Mashenka squatted in the dig site to examine the body. Kevin had retrieved the cameras from his tent. Mashenka looked up at him as he was adjusting the focus. "That reminds me, would you go into my tent and get my cell phone. I need the call to Sheriff's station."

Within the hour, Deputy Duncan arrived at the site. Kevin and Mashenka had continued to take pictures. They were looking for any identifying marks, Mashenka making notes as they go along. As Duncan moved closer to the gravesite, the stench of rotting human flesh filled the air. "What do you have so far?"

Mashenka stopped to inform Duncan of her findings just as she was about to pull the hair away from the back of the neck. "You've got pen and paper ready, or a tape recorder because I've got a lot of information for you."

Duncan reached into his jacket pocket and pulled out a small hand held recorder. He pressed the button to record. "Testing.... Testing 1 2 3." He stopped it, rewound, and pressed play to hear the same message back. Then he recorded a new message. "Case #02-00034, Body found at old Shelton farm house off of Beaujean Road just past the Crawford junction. Today's date March 15th, 2007, time 1445. Preliminary findings of Dr. Mashenka Vascovich." He nodded his head to indicate for her to start speaking.

Without hesitating Mashenka began her preliminary report. "Due to the amount of or should I say the lack of decay, I would say the body has been here for around four months. That would put the victim's death around November, 2006. The victim was bound and gagged at the time of her demise, probably with duct tape. The victim has some cuts and abrasions on the ankles, wrists, nap of the neck, and waist line indicating all clothing and tape were removed before burial, probably with a hunting knife. The clothing was probably removed first. She was taken to the edge of the gravesite and shot once in the back of the head with what appears to be a .45. She was then dropped, or pushed into the grave face down then the tape removed. Note that the victim is missing the ring finger on her left hand; this would indicate a wedding ring, or one of value, or easily identified ring. I say *she* because of the hip structure and frame of the body. I will need to take x-ray's of the body to get an accurate determination of age, but I'd say she was in her mid-twenties, about 5 foot 3, 110 to 115 pounds, black hair. Her eye color is most likely brown, but to be confirmed later. The next step is to roll the body over hopefully intact. That's currently all I have for now." Duncan stopped recording. Mashenka continued, "A pretty damn brutal killing, I'd say."

Duncan unlatched the case to his camera so he could start photographing the body. Mashenka stepped back to allow Duncan some clear camera shots. As Duncan snapped pictures she hypothesized, "I have a feeling we are going to find more of the same when we roll her over."

When Duncan was done, Mashenka signaled Kevin over to the body. Kevin was ready for the next phase. He carried over a white sheet, body bag, and three flat shovels in his hands. He placed all but the sheet down, then tucked the sheet under the body in the dirt with great care, and spread it out on the ground. The two students held the sheet to catch the body as Mashenka, Kevin, and Duncan each took a shovel and placed it in the dirt at a 45-degree angle to the body. Using the shovels as levers, they rolled the body over on to the sheet in one swift movement. Mashenka and Kevin took ordinary paintbrushes to clear away the dirt. Mashenka signaled Duncan to turn the recorder back on. "The body is now facing up. It is definitely female. It appears all her teeth have been removed to further prevent identification. No noticeable identification marks such as scars or birthmarks. That's it for now." With the recorder now off Mashenka continued, "We have to bag every thing up now. I've called for a refrigeration truck to transport the body to the university. I'll fax any updates as I get them to your office. You better get your pictures now." Kevin was already wrapping up his end of the picture taking.

The next step was to bag the body and place it in the pine box with the dry ice. Shipping the dirt and the body to the University was the easy part. The meticulous examination of the body and sifting through the dirt was going to be a long and arduous task.

The Connection

The humidity hung in the air, which felt more like steam from the shower. This August was the worst heat wave in years. Even with a dehumidifier, the sticky air made Detective Richardson less than amicable to be around. He had been antsy at home so he decided to go into work on his day off. Whenever he had some free time, which was not often, Richardson would go over an old evidence file. This file consisted of information he collected on a case he had worked on for over two years. It was marked closed. Closed due to the lack of any real physical evidence or any first hand witnesses. He knew, he just knew, Michael McCarron was somehow involved with the 'Mexican Mafia.' He just could not prove it. He had been close, so close he could taste it. He had a witness who was willing to go 'state's evidence,' but the day they were to pick up their snitch the witness had disappeared. The safe house was ready, but remained empty of his only connection to one of the largest, most violent drug cartels to ever hit the streets. People disappearing and dead bodies were not uncommon when it came to the cartel. Every time there was a breaking story on the cartel, he scoured it, looking for any name, which might sound familiar, looking for a name, which did not sound Hispanic.

The first article in his pile was regarding a large drug bust in Texas. On the boarders of Laredo, the boarder patrol had seized 1,200 pounds of cocaine from a pickup truck. The cocaine was stuffed into 16 duffel bags, which were hidden behind seats and in a toolbox of the pickup which also was seized. The $60 million load was pressed into hundreds of plastic-wrapped bricks which carried labels featuring Christmas trees and the words *Feliz Navidad*, Spanish for Merry Christmas. It was reported, "It was probably going to be repackaged and sent on to New York or Chicago."

The second article was more recent. In February, police arrested 10 men who they believed to be the overlords of a Southern California narcotics trafficking ring associated with Mexico's feared Tijuana drug cartel. They were known for hiring upper-class Mexicans in Tijuana. They had even reached into the San Diego area to find their young assassins known as 'narco-juniors.' Again, they recruited from the better neighborhoods. A neighborhood like the one Michael was from.

The first time he encountered Michael was at a college bar near NYU at Buffalo. He thought he was a small time hood and tried to recruit him as a snitch. What he got was disinformation, leads which eventually lead nowhere and leads which usually took them in the wrong direction. Richardson, after much insistence had received the go ahead to run surveillance on Michael. He received court approval to do a wiretap on his phone. Months went by before he listened in on a conversation which struck him as odd. The entire conversation was in Spanish. His knowledge of the language was little to none, but it was obvious Michael had full command of the language. He had the recording translated and discovered there was a shipment coming in the next night. The department assigned him an undercover cop who was fluent in Spanish. He was just a young kid, only 24 years old, but he was street smart.

The night of the anticipated drop they went in with full back up of Buffalo's finest. A small abandoned warehouse was surrounded. As they secured the building an explosion rocked it when they entered an interior door. The kid never knew what hit him. He had taken the brunt of a focused blast. Richardson had held him in his arms while he breathed his last breath of life. That was almost two years ago. Yet, the memory haunted him every day. Richardson hounded Michael from that day forward. Michael McCarron was not going to breathe without him knowing. Once his prime witness had disappeared, Richardson had demanded the DA request a postponement on the hearing of evidence for drug trafficking. The DA did not like being told what to do. He had examined what evidence there was, and then made a weak case for postponement. The case was dismissed. Michael McCarron walked out of the courthouse with his high priced lawyer. He glared at Richardson as he walked by. Then he stopped to speak, "You're not smart enough to bring me down." That was the last Richardson had seen, or heard of him. Try as he might to find him, Michael had disappeared into thin air.

This latest article from the LA Times, which he held in his hand, listed only Spanish sounding names. He placed the clipping in the ever-growing folder, closed it, and left it resting on his desk. Sitting back in his chair, he stared at it, almost willing it to divulge some magical information he had not already read over a hundred times. Every article, every report had nothing but Spanish surnames for the arrested parties. Yet, he knew Michael was involved. His witness had told him so. No magic today. So, Richardson packed the folder up and placed it back into the drawer. He proceeded to close the drawer when a paper from another folder was caught then pulled up. He tried to straighten the paper out to slide it back into its folder when he decided to take it out and look at it. He had forgotten about Katie's fax so he read it over again.

Renter: John Talbert.

References: Jorge Quinteros, Alan Lundgren, and Mary Barton.

Emergency: Jack Richardson.

So far this was the only piece of paper he had associated with a violent crime which had a mix of Spanish and European surnames not to mention his own name. Deciding a long shot was better than a dead end street, he called the number on the message pad.

"Hi, is this Katie? This is Jack Richardson with the Buffalo PD, narcotics division… Yeah, that's right… Uh huh… Did you ever find the Jack Richardson on that app you faxed me?… No huh, how about the perp? Do you have any leads on him? No? You've obtained a basic description on the perp and on the victim? Do me a favor, fax me what you have. I'll look it over. If I come up with something, I'll give you a call… Great… yes that fax number is correct. I'll be waiting right by the machine… Yeah, I'm doing fine. Looking forward to a month's vacation…in a couple of weeks… Nope, don't have anywhere special planned. How 'bout you?… Good… Good… Oh yes, your sister's wedding... Tell her congratulations for me, will you? Oh, I hear the fax coming through right now. Nice talking to you."

Jack hung up the phone and walked over to the fax machine to retrieve the incoming fax. Sixteen pages later, the machine stopped spewing out paper. He read over the description of "John Talbert." It fit, not exactly, but it was close enough. He removed the thick folder back out of the drawer and thumbed through the papers until he came across the mug shots taken of Michael. Picking the phone up, he redialed Katie.

"Katie, I have some mug shots of a guy who sort of fits the description. He's not balding like your guy, but he is the around the same age, height, stature and coloring...Yeah, I know it's fast on my part. I've been looking for this scum for a while. Do you have an e-mail address?...ah huh...yeah, I've got it. I'll scan these pictures and e-mail them to you. It shouldn't take more than 15-20 minutes. Maybe this Mr. Shelton will recognize him...Yeah, wouldn't that be great...No I haven't looked at the description of the victim yet...Yeah, I see that. Eight pages of the gruesome details...Sure, sure I'll give her a call if I think of anything. What's her name?... How do you spell that V-A-S-C-O-V-I-C-H, the number at the University? Ah huh, yep I got it. Thanks Katie. I'll get that over to you right away."

Jack handed over the mug shots to the floor's master computer wizard to scan and e-mail the color photos out. Then he returned to his desk, and scanned over the victim's description. Without any hesitation, he picked the phone up and called the University.

"Ms. Vascovich, This is Jack Richardson with the Buffalo PD. The Chautauqua County Sheriff's Department contacted me regarding the body you excavated in Mayville. I was wondering if you had located any tattoos on the body...No...Did you look under the hair, back of the head behind the victims left ear...Not yet, would it be possible to do so and give me a call back...Well, I've been looking for a missing witness for about ten months now. From what the Sheriff's department faxed me, this body fits a general description... Good. I'll be waiting for your call."

Jack decided to fetch himself a cup of coffee. He never liked the hurry up and wait game, but he was used to it. As he walked back towards his desk, he stopped by the computer wizard's desk. "Tom, did you send off those pictures?"

Tom peered up from his monitor. "Sure did. It took a while. I had a slow connection. Sure, wish the department would allocate funds for a T1 connection, but I guess it's low on their priority, right under chairs that don't wobble and break." He tried to adjust the backrest of his chair which persisted to fall down to the lowest position again. "What are you working on?"

Jack stared off in the direction of his desk hoping the phone would ring.

"Hope and a miracle, Tom, a hope and a miracle."

His phone did ring out and he dashed over to pick it up. "Richardson...Hello, Shelley." Shelley was his ex-wife. They had met in college and married in their second year. Jack got his BA and dropped out of the masters program to join the police force. Shelley went on to get her master's in business administration. She could not handle the hours Jack worked, or worrying about him coming home in a body bag. He started out working some of the worst areas of Buffalo. Then when he went into narcotics, she said she could not take it anymore and left.

He could not blame her. Jack knew he was more dedicated to his job than his marriage. Now she was married to a real estate broker. They had three kids and she was miserable. Of course, she was always miserable, always complaining about something. There were times he wished he had severed all connections with Shelley, times like now.

"Oh, so you and the dick had another fight did ya? Well, this is a big surprise?… I'm sorry Shelley, I just don't understand why you call me every time you two have a fight. There's nothing I can do to make it better…No I'm not a good listener, I've never been a good listener. You've reminded me of that at least a hundred times while we were married…. Don't you have other friends, your mother, anyone you can talk to? Like a therapist?…Yeah, you're right, I'm not in a very good mood." Call waiting beeped in his ear. "Shelley, I've got another call…Shelley I have to go this maybe important…Yes, you're important too, but I have to go." He slammed the phone down then waited for it to ring. It did not ring. Frustrated, he ran his fingers through what little hair he had left on the top of his head. "Ah, shit! Come on call back."

The phone rang and he snatched it up before it completed the ring.

"Richardson." He barked out.

Mashenka had been working late as usual. She too had been going over the case notes to see if she could eek out some new clue to the case. Richardson's call had breathed new hope to a possible conclusion to this body's identity. Upon reexamining the body, she promptly called him back.

"Hi, this is Mashenka. I thought I'd call you right away to let you know what I found. You were right on about the tattoo. It's small and almost indistinguishable now, but it's there. Your missing witness, what kind of tattoo did she have?"

Jack already had his folder open to the page of notes obtained from his snitch. "She said it was her boyfriend's initials sort of in the shape of a butterfly. It's a double M with a small S in the middle. Is that what you found?" Jack found he was not breathing waiting for Mashenka to reply.

"Yeah, I'd say that fits the description exactly. So do we have a name for this poor woman now?"

He really did not have to read his notes again. Every detail about this woman was etched in his mind forever.

"Aurora Marie Gutierrez-Sandoval. She was a Mexican illegal who hooked up with one Michael McCarron. She disappeared last November and he in December after the charges were dropped. I've sent pictures of Michael to the Sheriff's Department, so maybe I'll get lucky twice in one day."

Mashenka wrote down Jane Doe's new name with a question mark, meaning she needed confirmation. "Well, Ms. Sandoval here wasn't so lucky. Your Michael McCarron took great care to make sure there was little, or no evidence to be found. I ran a full toxicology on her. She was so pumped up with barbiturates and cocaine she probably didn't even know what was going on. I figure he drugged her up, placed her in the bathtub where he proceeded to remove all her teeth with pliers then removed her fingertips with the kind of clippers used on thick rose bushes. By the time he took her outside to finish the job the pain, shock, and drugs made her death seem like a mercy killing. We never did find her clothing, teeth, or fingertips, but we did find the casing to a .45 in the excavated dirt. Somehow, he missed that, or he left it on purpose to show us how clever he could be. How did you get involved in being notified on this case?"

Richardson sighed, "It appears he put my name down on a renter's application as an emergency contact. He had told me once that I wasn't smart enough to bring him down, and right now I feel like he wasn't too far off the mark."

Mashenka responded to him with a kind tone in her voice. She could tell he was disturbed that the perpetrator had appeared to have bested him. "Well, he certainly has an ego. That may be his Achilles heel, the very thing that will bring him down. I'll bring all this information to the shrink and have him add it to the profile. Maybe you *will* get lucky twice in one day. Then all we have to do is find him. I always look forward to seeing these bastards go down for the count."

Jack felt a knot in his stomach and reached for the anti-acids. He poured out a small handful from the bottle and popped them into his mouth.

"If I was a praying man I'd be down on my knees right now begging God for a break in this case. Thanks for all your help. I'll give you a call if I get my miracle."

Jack sat around the office until around six o'clock then decided to get some Chinese food and go home. The hurry up and wait game sometimes drove him crazy.

Entering his apartment, Jack threw his keys down on the counter. He removed a rented DVD from a bag and placed it in the player. Sitting down on the couch with his container of Chinese food, he found his food had already turned cold. While the pre-movie footage played out, he took the container and placed it in the microwave setting the timer for two minutes then pressed start. As he stood at the microwave, he noticed the light blinking on his answering machine. He rewound it and then pressed play. Four hang-ups, one message from Shelley saying she and the dick had kissed and made up, and one message to call the office. The microwave dinged as to say, "all done." He removed the container of food out and proceeded to eat and dial at the same time.

"Richardson here, I understand you have a message for me."

The desk officer working the night shift thumbed through a stack of messages. He located the one marked Richardson and read back the message.

"Katie from the Chautauqua County Sheriff's called saying the confirmation on the pictures was high. The Sheltons did not get home until late, a funeral or something. So, they had to wait to show them the mug shots. Says here they have contacted the FBI and need to have the rap sheet. I took the liberty of faxing the information that we had in our computers, sir. She was very excited about all of this, said this was the best day of her life. Especially since a Ma shane ka Vas ko vhich notified her on the body's possible identity. She sure does like to talk. I didn't write it all down, but that's the general gist of the conversation. Do you want her number?"

Jack rubbed his beard thinking about the day, "No, that's okay. I'll call her tomorrow. Thanks."

It had been a long day, a productive day, a day of hopes and miracles. Now he had to let it all sink in and decide what to do next. Michael McCarron was no longer under Buffalo PD's jurisdiction. The one thing he had to figure out was how to have the department allow him to be involved in the case. First, things first, eat, relax, and then sleep. Tomorrow would take care of itself.

The Brewing Tempest

Matt had pilfered twelve of Laura's paintings out of the house and had arranged to meet with Dave at a local restaurant. They had again been conspiring to surprise Laura. This time Dave had decided to mat and frame some of Laura's artwork. He was even trying to get a local gallery to display her work. Her birthday was coming up in a month, and he wanted enough time to have one of the guys he worked with complete the project. Matt found Dave seated in a booth next to the window, coffee on the table and newspaper hiding his face. As he sat down across from Dave, he lowered the newspaper. "Got them." Matt had a big grin on his face. "I went through them last night while you two were out to dinner. I picked out the ones I know she likes the best. There's twelve. That's not too many is it?"

Dave folded and laid the paper down on the seat next to him. "No, no that sounds perfect. Come on let me see which ones you have."

Matt placed the cardboard folder on the tabletop. Dave opened it slightly and looked at the paintings inside. Matt was amused at how cautious Dave was being.

"She's not here. You can go ahead and take a good look."

Dave gingerly examined which paintings Matt had brought to him. "I don't want anything to get on them. I'd feel awful if anything happened to them." Dave closed the folder and placed it on the seat next to him, on top of his newspaper. "Shall we celebrate a job well done? Breakfast is on me."

Matt inspected the menu before him, "Cool, I'm starved. Mom is going to be so jazzed. This was a great idea. Have I ever said 'Thank you' for everything you've done? You know I've never seen my mother as happy as she has been this last year."

The waitress interrupted them to take their order. "You boys ready to order now?"

Matt looked up at her to see a tired older woman trying to put on a smile for her tip. "Yeah, I'll have the number three breakfast, over easy with sour dough toast and coffee."

"And you, honey, what will you have?" She directed towards Dave.

"I'll have the chicken fried steak with extra gravy, scrambled, whole wheat, and more coffee."

"Coming right up, sugar."

Dave and Matt handed her the menus, and she gave them a wink before she left. Matt curled up his lip in disgust.

"Gross, she was flirting with you."

"Nah, I think she was flirting with you." Dave taunted.

Matt slumped back into his seat. "Ah Dave, that's obscene. That woman was old enough to be my mother, my grandmother."

Dave laughed with delight, "But it's so much fun to watch you squirm at the mere thought of it…and you're welcome. When it comes to your mother and you boys, it's all a labor of love."

Matt and Dave sat and talked as they ate their breakfast before going off to school and work respectively.

It had been almost a year since Dave and Laura's paths had crossed. Kismet, it was kismet. He knew in his heart they were meant to be together. At long last, he finally found the woman he planned on marrying. He looked forward to spending the rest of their lives growing old together.

It was around four o'clock in the afternoon. Laura had taken off work early to get the cat from the vets. He was none too happy about it either. She removed the carrier from her car and entered the house. Expecting to find no one home, she was surprised to hear music coming from Kyle's room. She placed the carrier on the counter and opened the door so Newt could run free. "There you go. Now no more sneaking out of the house and no more cat fights, you hear?" Newt jumped down from the counter to inspect his food dish. "I thought having you fixed would stop all this nonsense."

The music got louder as Kyle came out from his room. The smell of cigarette smoke mixed with weed emanated from his room. He strolled from his room to the bathroom not even aware Laura was there. She decided to stand in front of the door so he could not miss her on his way out. Kyle opened the door, and his eyes had the look of shock and fear.

"You scared me half to death. What are you doing home so early?"

Laura had her arms crossed in front of her, "I want to know the same thing about you. What are you doing home? Why aren't you at work?"

Kyle became belligerent, "I quit. It was a shit job. They were always having me do shit work. No big loss. I'll find another job."

Laura went into full sarcasm, "Oh, no big loss, you'll find another job. You never found this one. It found you. No job, no home. How do you like that little piece of reality? I'll not have you sitting around here doing nothing. You can go stay at your girlfriend's house since you're there most of the time anyway. See how long they'll put up with you lying around their house."

Kyle stared at her in dismay, "You wouldn't do that to your own kid."

Laura stepped in so her face was right in his. Then she took a good whiff of his breath. "Bet me, you violated my trust for the last time. You quit your job without having another one lined up and worse yet, you're smoking dope in my house. Therefore, you have two choices. Pack up your things and leave, or I call the police and let them search your room. So what is it going to be?"

Kyle snatched up the phone and handed it to her, "Fuck you. You don't have the balls."

She grabbed the phone from his hand, "No, if I had balls you would have been out of here a long time ago." She started to dial 911, but before she could press the last number, Kyle snatched the phone away from her and pushed her away. Laura backed up suddenly afraid of her own son.

Kyle dialed his girlfriend's number. "Megan, Come and get me. MOTHER just kicked me out of the house…I don't know, we'll figure that out later. Just come and get me." He slammed the phone down. Filled with hate and anger he snapped, "Don't worry, Mother dear. I'll be out of this palace in about an hour." Kyle returned to his room and slammed the door.

Laura could hear him opening and closing closet doors and Chester-drawers from the other room. The idea of being alone in the house with Kyle as angry as he was frightened her. She picked up the phone to call Dave at the job site. The phone rang about ten times before anyone picked up. Grace breathlessly answered the phone, "Rucker Construction. This is Grace. Can I help you?"

Laura was glad Nick did not answer. She was sure he would not be too happy about Kyle walking off the job.

"Hi, Grace. This is Laura. Is Dave still there?"

Grace had been walking down the steps heading for her car when the phone rang. She still had purse and keys in hand.

"No, Laura, he's not. He left about a half hour ago, right after he found out about Kyle. I think he said he was heading towards your place. Something about wanting to get there before you did and talk some sense into the boy. I hope that helps. You sure do have your hands full with that kid."

Laura took a deep breath then exhaled, "Yeah, I know. I'll keep my eye out for him. He should be here anytime now. Thanks Grace." Laura made her way out to the front porch and sat on the stairs. She rested her elbows on her knees with her head in her hands. Tears rolled down her face and dropped on the step below her. The inevitable had finally happened. She had hoped and prayed things would change, that Kyle would change. Maybe, he would grow up and somehow, the old Kyle, the Kyle she loved and remembered would return. Now all hopes and prayers dashed against the step with each tear.

Dave's truck screeched around the corner then headed straight for Laura's house. He parked the wrong way on the street, in front of the stairs. Dave jumped out of the truck and sat down next to her wrapping his arm around her shoulder. Laura looked up at him with mascara running down her face.

"I told him to get out. There were angry, mean words said and now I guess he's packing. Either that or he's destroying his room.... I'm glad you're here. I...I was afraid to be alone with my own son. God help me I was afraid." She leaned into his body and he wrapped both arms around her. She sobbed softly.

Dave kissed the top of her head and stroked her hair. "Kyle won't do anything while I'm here. Do you know where he's going?"

She responded without looking up, "Yeah, Megan's. She should be here pretty soon."

Dave stood up and he placed his hand out for her to take. "Come on, let's go inside. It's your home. Don't let him banish you outside. It makes it seem like he won."

They ambled back inside. Laura grabbed some tissues from the counter and wiped her eyes. A car pulled up across the street and honked the horn. Kyle exited the house without a word, without further incident. She leaned back against the kitchen counter; her hands held the tissue against her mouth and her chest heaved as she tried to hold back the tears. Dave again took her into his arms and she wept uncontrollably.

The following weekend Dave, Laura, Matt, and Alicen decided they needed some get away time. They packed up the truck with fishing and camping equipment and headed towards San Elijo State Beach located in Encinitas. Matt and Alicen sat uncomfortably in the extended cab area of Dave's truck. After more than an hours drive, they finally set up camp. The women shared the larger of the two tents.

It was a beautiful September morning. There was a slight breeze in the air. The cool salty wind felt good on Laura's face as the sun countered the coolness with its warm rays. The men had gone into the little store to purchase bait appropriate for the current fishing. Alicen and Laura leaned over the railing at the campsite to look down over the cliffs at the ocean below. It was going to be good fishing. They could actually see the fish in the surf below. Dave and Matt came back with containers of squid, clams, something they called Blood Worms, and brightly colored artificial bait. Matt snatched two of the fishing poles, the tackle box, and a folding chair. Dave grabbed two more poles, a day cooler, and a folding chair.

"Come on girls the fish await." Matt said with excitement.

"You see those silly grins on their faces. You'd think they were six years old going on their first fishing trip." Alicen said as she picked up the remaining two chairs, one in each hand.

Laura picked up the bag of groceries off the picnic table, battened down her hat, and walked towards the stairs leading down to the ocean.

"You heard the boys, 'The fish await.' You know this is payback for all the PMS bull they've had to put up with from us women."

Several flights of stairs later they found an area on the beach, which was far away from the surfers and all other people. Laura and Alicen sat in their beach chairs with their poles wedged into the sand, and supported by rocks. They watched as Dave and Matt waded in the surf, casting their lines out in hope of a big catch. The waves kept pounding them as they stood in the surf. Occasionally a large wave would hit them about chest high. While Dave tried to cast his line out, a particularly large wave blasted him, filling his waders full of water. Alicen yelled out, "That was a good one Dad. Maybe you should check your boots for a fish since they don't seem to like our bait."

Weighted down with water, Dave struggled to come into shore with his pole in tow. He laid the pole down and undid his suspenders then proceeded to peal the waders off to expose sopping wet clothing. "Are you sure you girls saw fish in the surf from all the way up there?" He squinted his eyes, as he looked up the cliff to the top where the girls said the saw they fish from the railing, with a doubtful eye.

Laura made a cross sign over her heart, "Cross my heart and swear to die, if I lie."

Dave gave her a disapproving look, "I hate that expression." He scratched his head, "Maybe I should try different bait."

Sitting in the sand, he opened the bag with the recently purchased bait. Matt abruptly yelled out, "Hey you guys. I caught a fish. What kind of fish, I don't know. Not a very big fish, but a fish none the less."

Matt strode into shore with his pole in one hand and the line with the flopping fish in the other like a proud hunter. He stood in front of them holding up his prize. "Well, anyone bring a camera to capture this moment?"

Alicen giggled as she looked upon the maybe six-inch catch of the day. "Surely you jest. I think a picture of this event would be used more for blackmail than a trophy memento."

Matt proudly stood erect, "Oh quite contraire, Madame. You see this is my very first time fishing and my very first fish. Therefore, I am a natural. With a little practice it will only be a matter of time before Moby Dick is begging to be at the end of *my* pole."

Alicen bowed her head, "I'm sorry kind sir. I did not mean to make light of such a momentous occasion. Please forgive me." They both giggled. Matt undid the fish from its hook, and then he ran to the surfs edge to release the creature. "Be free to live yet another day." The fish flopped in the water then swam away.

That evening, they all sat around the fire ring in full flame. They were each holding a long stick with hot dogs roasting on the end. Laura removed her stick from the flames. She brought the hot dogs up to her face and blew out the red ember at the end of the stick, then she broke off a piece of the burnt hot dog and ate it. "I think we should have brought something more than just hot dogs, chips, and s'mores. I mean just in case we didn't catch any fish. I mean I was looking forward to something like poached salmon, not...not hot dogs."

Dave stared into the fire as one of his hot dogs fell off into the flames. "Nope, no salmon here. Not in these waters. How about this, if I don't catch us a big...I mean a big fish tomorrow, I'll take us all to dinner, deal?"

They all squealed in unison, "Deal!"

Alicen chirped up, "At least we will get one good meal out of this trip."

Dave gave her a slightly crossed eyed gaze for her remark. Laura placed her hand on Dave's arm and smiled. "Thanks. I'm having a really, really good time. You always seem to know how to bring me out of the dumps, to help me see the good things in life. You're a good man."

Dave took hold of Laura's hand. "I could do nothing less for the best thing that ever happened to me."

Matt fetched soda out of the cooler. Politely he asked, "Anyone else like one?" Heads nodded yes and Matt tossed a soda to Dave who in turn handed it to Laura. They all sat around the fire pit for hours talking until the fire dwindled down and the cool ocean air bit through their clothes. It was a clear night and the heavens unfolded their beauty. Laura and Alicen retired to their tent leaving the men contemplating the origin and meaning of life while watching the stars, looking for asteroids, and other such things. In other words, 'men talk.'

On the trip home, Dave had found a nice little bar, which served a good meal for the money. It was around five thirty Sunday evening when they were preparing to leave the restaurant. As he stood at the counter near the cash register waiting to pay the bill, he glanced up at the television located above the bar. The picture staring back at him made him take pause. Alicen snuggled up next to him and placed her arm in his. "Thanks for the great fish dinner, Dad. The catch of the day was superb." Still staring at the television he asked, "Do you have a pen and paper?" Then to the bartender, "Could you turn the sound up on that?" Alicen searched her purse for a pen and a piece of paper. "What's going on? What's got you entranced here?" Dave signaled her to wait a minute. "Shh... let me listen."

The TV announcer is heard. "Ladies and Gentlemen, before we leave you tonight, we would like you to take a look at the pictures behind me. This man here has just been placed on our most wanted list. He goes by the name of Michael McCarron or John Talbert. He is a 24-year-old Caucasian, 5'11", 160 lbs, red hair, and blue eyes. He is suspected of kidnapping, murder, and drug trafficking. He is considered extremely dangerous. Anyone, having any knowledge as to his whereabouts, please contact us at the number listed at the bottom of the screen. That concludes tonight's episode of 'America's Most Wanted.' We'll see you next time."

Dave scribbled down the telephone number on a piece of paper. Alicen, concerned with her father's actions, continued with her questions. "Dad, what's going on? Who was that guy?" Dave folded the paper and placed it carefully in his wallet. "Hopefully nothing, hon. That guy just looked awfully familiar, that's all. Nothing to worry your pretty little head about." He gave her a comforting kiss on her forehead.

After the cashier finished with another customer, she made her way to the register. She rang up the ticket and then ran Dave's credit card through her machine. She handed him back his card with the receipt for him to sign. "Saw you locked into the tube there for a moment. That's my favorite program too. I keep waiting to see my sister's boyfriend's face pop up on that screen."

Dave scribbled his signature on the receipt and handed it back to her. "I don't think I've ever seen that program before. Here you go. I added in the tip."

The cashier looked at the receipt. "Thank you sir. You have a real nice day."

Dave placed his arm around Alicen's shoulder, "Come on Sunshine, let's round up Matt and Laura. We still have a ways to go before we reach home."

They all met up outside, and then piled back into the truck. The ride home seemed longer than forty-five minutes. Dave was unusually quiet. Laura thought it was just because he was tired, but Alicen knew what he had seen on that program weighed heavy on his mind. She thought she would talk to him about it later.

***

The sound of the sander grinding against the metal of the car echoed for blocks as Sean stripped the orange paint from his 68 Dodge Super Bee. It had been a quiet morning until then. Ramón staggered out the front door onto the run down creaking porch of the rented old house in Rubidoux. Upon seeing Ramón's sorry sight, Sean stopped the sander. Ramón leaned against the pillar at the entry to the porch, wearing blue jeans and a white t-shirt. Unshaven and his hair standing on end, he ran his fingers like a comb through his hair then rubbed his forehead and eyes with the palm of his hands.

"You got any aspirin? I've got a horrible headache."

Sean acted as though Ramón had not spoken and took a piece of sandpaper from off the ground to remove the missed specks of paint. Then he blew on the spot to see the metal glisten clean. He cocked his head to gaze upon a very sorry sight.

"I believe it's called a hangover, Ramón. You're such a dick. With all the work and preparation we need to do, all you can think about is drinking and screwing. Serves you right. I hope you feel like your fuckin' brains are going to explode."

Just to annoy Ramón, Sean started up the sander again and Ramón wandered back into the house to find the much-needed aspirin. The small house was filthy. The living room contained a mattress pushed up against the wall, a old black and white TV with rabbit ears that was sitting on a straight back chair about three feet away from the mattress. The kitchen had a cardboard table, two chairs, a small gas stove, a refrigerator which did not work, and counters filled with various car parts. The sink contained a single dirty drinking glass. The cupboards were bare. Ramón made his way to the bathroom, which smelled of urine. He looked at himself in the mirror and scraped his tongue with his teeth, making a face like he just tasted something disgusting. He opened the medicine cabinet to find a toothbrush and tooth paste which had leaked all over the shelf, and a bottle of aspirin. Taking the lid off, he dumped eight of them into the palm of his hand then popped them in his mouth. Turning on the water, he bent down to the faucet to slurp some water so he could swallow the pills. Then he dunked his head under the flow of water as best he could to wet his hair and rinse his face. Again, he combed back his hair with his fingers. There were no towels in sight so he wiped his hands on his jeans and headed back outside to the antagonistic sound of the sander.

Sean had been working on his pride and joy for over six months. It had been his sole project since he was fired from the construction site. Ramón took a seat on the porch steps.

"Your house is a pig sty. You ever going to be done with that piece of shit? Do you even have it running?"

Sean sprayed the sanded down area with a can of gray primer. "For a guy that was too hung over to go to work you sure have a lot of annoying questions. For your information, yes, she runs. This piece of shit, as you called it, has a 426 Hemi engine, dual exhausts, heavy-duty drive shaft, a 4-speed transmission with a Hurst shifter. This baby can outrun anything out there."

Ramón strolled over to where Sean was working. He touched the gray primer and shook his head. "What I can't figure out is why you sanded that beautiful paint job off."

Moving him out of the way, Sean continued to spray paint. "You know with a master mind like yours I'm amazed that you're still a free man. You ever heard of being inconspicuous. I know that's a big word for a third grade drop out like you, but did you ever think bright orange paint might attract a lot of attention? Gray on the other hand kind of disappears, makes you invisible."

Ramón always hated it when Sean would put him down. "Hey, you know I got my diploma." He raised the hood of the car to take a look at Sean's pride and joy. "A 426 Hemi, huh? How about you show me what she can do."

Sean pleased to show off his hard work was more than willing to give Ramón a little thrill ride, but first, he needed to know if Ramón had acquired the information, he asked for.

"Well, that all depends Ramón. Did you get those addresses I asked for?" Ramón stood there with a blank look on his face. "Earth to Major Tom. The addresses? Isn't that why you were out last night?"

Ramón nervously started searching his pockets. "Yeah, Yeah, I have it. I just don't remember where I put it. But, it's okay. I remember the one and Javier got the other two for me. All I have to do is make a phone call and…" He pulled a folded up bar napkin out of his back pocket. "Here it is. See, here it is. I wouldn't let you down. You gave me a job to do and I did it. See?"

Sean snapped the napkin out of his hand. He held it out at a distance then back close to his face, trying to read what Ramón had written. "I'm supposed to be able to read this? God Ramón, you write like a drop out. And, it's all blurry like you got it wet. What good is this going to do if I can't read it?"

Ramón held his hand out for Sean to give it back. "Here let me have it. I can read it. I'll go inside and rewrite it real good for you. Okay? No problem I'll take care of it. Just tell me where to find a pencil and paper."

With a doubtful eye, he returned the napkin to him. "There's some paper in a drawer next to the sink in the kitchen. Just make sure I can read it and they better be right."

Ramón set off toward the house mumbling about appeasing the 'Sean God.' Sean returned the sander to the front driver's side fender. It was the last panel to have the remaining orange paint removed. A few minutes later Ramón handed Sean the rewritten addresses.

"Here, is this better?"

Sean examined the paper to determine if he could decipher Ramón's chicken scratch. "Yeah, it'll do. Come on I'll take you for a spin." Sean very meticulously folded the paper into a square and placed it in his wallet which he returned to his pant pocket. He then slid through the driver's side window behind the steering wheel. Ramón ran to the other side of the car to jump in just as Sean slammed the Super Bee into first gear. He peeled out and headed down the gravel road towards town and the freeway.

Ramón searched for a seat belt and found none so he held onto the passenger door. "Shit, this baby has power." Sean stepped on the pedal to demonstrate she still had a lot more. Ramón was forced back into the seat.

"I still don't get why you needed those addresses."

Sean observed Ramón holding on for dear life. He grinned, seeing the fear in his face. "It's just an insurance policy, just in case someone decides to stick their nose where it doesn't belong."

As he turned onto a main access road, he saw a cop car pull into the truck stop just ahead. Down shifting, he slowed the car down to the speed limit. They passed by the truck stop, never taking their eyes off the patrol car. The officer exited his vehicle and headed for the restaurant. Ramón breathed a sigh of relief and relaxed into the seat.

"That reminds me. Yesterday, when I was leaving work there was a suit talking to that Dave guy. Don't think he was a local, looked more like a fed."

At this point, Sean gripped the steering wheel and stepped on the gas making a sharp turn back onto a gravel road, nearly loosing control of the car. He pulled the car out of the fish tail then slammed on the brakes. Ramón was thrown into the dashboard, hitting his head. He sat back up and rubbed his forehead with his hand. As he pulled his hand back down, he noticed blood.

"Jesus H Christ Sean, are you trying to kill me?"

Sean reached under the seat and pulled out the .45. He placed it to Ramón's temple and pulled back the trigger. "No asshole, if I was going to kill you, I'd just pull the trigger and dump your body right here."

Ramón pressed his body into the door, trying to move as far away as possible. "What! What did I do?"

Sean un-cocked the .45 and scratched his head with the barrel. "Were you just born stupid, or do you have to work at it? I've been telling you for months to keep an eye out for cops snooping around. Then you risk leading them right to me."

Sean waved the gun in Ramón's face. Ramón's hands came up in front of his face. "I swear Sean. No one followed me. They didn't even see me. I could see them, but they couldn't see me. I swear on my mother's life."

Sean placed the gun back under the seat. He shifted into first gear to return to the house. "You know this changes everything now. You can't go back to the job site. It was just convenient to have you there on the premises. Besides, they'll start grilling you and to be perfectly honest, I don't trust you. Even if you thought you wouldn't say anything, you'd fuck up and tell them something that would mess up everything. Nope, you can't go back. Do they have a valid address on you?"

Ramón, thankful Sean had put the gun away, returned to nursing his wound. "What. What do you mean?"

Sean drove the car onto the front lawn of his house. "You are such a rock. Does Nick have a real address on file in your employment records?"

"Of course not. I'm not that stupid."

Sean exited his door, slammed it, and then leaned on the roof staring at Ramón. "Well sometimes that's a hard one to call."

***

Katie had called Detective Richardson as soon as she received the news that they had a response to the blip on 'America's Most Wanted.' He had been trying to figure out a way to get the captain to allow him to stay involved in the case with no luck. It had been more than three years since he had taken a vacation so he decided to submit for a month's worth. To his surprise, it was granted. Of course, he was sternly warned to stay away from the case and Michael McCarron in particular. So, for the first time in years he was donning short hair and was clean-shaven. He told everyone he was going to Idaho to check out some land prospects. They all knew he dreamed of building his retirement home on a secluded piece of property so no one suspected he was already en route to California. The flight had been uneventful. He was thankful no one had been seated next to him so he did not have to make small talk. He took this opportunity to go over his notes. Katie had informed him of the agent's name currently assigned to the case. She had also given him the name and address of the man who had called the hot line. Jack always could get women to spill their guts, but he almost felt guilty at how easy it was to get all the details from Katie.

It had been nearly eight hours since he had left Buffalo. The Ontario Airport was still bustling with arrivals and departures. The lay out of the airport was simple enough to follow. He had no problems locating his luggage, or the check-in counter for the car rental. As busy as it was, Jack wondered what kind of zoo the LA airport would have been at this hour and was glad he did not need to find out. At the rental car counter Jack noticed the clock on the wall. The clock read 2:10. He looked at his wristwatch, which he had not adjusted for the time zone. It read 5:10. The day wore heavy on him. He figured with a little luck he might get six hours sleep before he had to get up to meet with Agent Schroeder. He asked the clerk behind the counter for directions to the hotel. Fortunately, the hotel was only a couple of blocks away. Tomorrow was going to be a long and hopefully a productive day.

The wake up call came promptly at 8:00. He rolled over and blindly groped for the ringing phone. A mechanical voice announced his wake up time. He sat up on the edge of his bed and ran his fingers through his thinning hair. He quickly showered and shaved, and then dressed. Finding the number to the Riverside FBI field office, he picked up the phone and requested an outside line. He dialed the number from the small piece of paper he had pulled the out of his wallet. "Agent Schroeder, please." He was immediately put on hold. After what seemed to be an eternity, Agent Schroeder finally picked up the line. Jack confirmed their appointment and received directions to the local office.

"Okay, that's the 60 freeway to the 91 north and off at Fourteenth St. How long do you think this will take me, providing I don't get lost?… About thirty minutes at the most. Good, I'll see you around ten o'clock."

Jack stepped off the elevator onto the 5th floor of the building, which housed the local FBI office. His stomach growled for food. The hotel's continental breakfast was not going to hold him well. He walked down the corridor until he found suite number 523 and entered a small reception area. A glass window slid open. A gray haired woman peered out the window.

"Detective Richardson?"

"Yes, Ma'am"

"Come on in through that door. Agent Schroeder is expecting you."

The receptionist escorted him to a small unimpressive office. It was a barren office with a single picture of the president and a FBI certification on the wall. One file cabinet fitted squarely in the corner of the room. A fax machine and a paper shredder sat on a table behind the desk. The desk had a computer monitor, keyboard, and mouse. An uncomfortable straight back chair sat on the other side of his desk waiting for its next temporary guest or victim. Papers were strewn across the agent's desk. Agent Schroeder was busy making notes in a file in front of him.

Agent Schroeder was in his mid-fifties, standing about 5'10", just a little shorter than Jack. He had a physic of a man who probably played football in his heyday. His friends called him Duke because that is where he obtained his degree. He was a no-nonsense kind of guy, tenacious, and focused. Jack entered the room and extended his hand out to greet him.

"Agent Schroeder, it's a pleasure to meet you. I'm Jack…"

Schroeder signaled Jack to sit down and continued to write in the file before him.

"I know who you are Detective. I just got off the phone with your office in Buffalo. It appears you're not supposed to be here. I am temporarily going to ignore that fact because I feel you may have some information that *may* help us in apprehending this low life. I also understand your drive, your need to bring this man down. So, as long as you are a benefit to this case and me you can stay. As soon as you're not, you're outta here. Now, I did not inform your office of our meeting here today, but…" Schroeder finished writing his notes, closed the file, and looked up to where Jack was seated. He stared momentarily. "You bear an uncanny resemblance to the man who called in the tip."

Jack took a moment to allow this last sentence to register. "This man who called in the tip, did he have any direct contact with the perp?"

Schroeder was still staring at him, making Jack more than a little uncomfortable. Schroeder finally responded to his question, "Yeah, he worked with him. In fact, he was responsible for his release from his job. Not to mention the perp scared the hell out of his girlfriend once."

Quickly Jack assessed the situation, not liking his conclusion. "If that is true, Agent Schroeder, I fear this man and his family's lives could be in danger. I think you know I relentlessly pursued Michael McCarron for over two years trying to build a case against him. From what I read in his psychological profile he not only doesn't have both oars in the water, he has his boat on a different planet. He could easily perceive this man as a threat, that threat being me. Could we go talk to him?"

Schroeder opened the upper right hand drawer to his desk. He removed his car keys. "I think you could be right. That would explain the hostility your Michael McCarron has displayed towards this guy right from the get go. By the way, he goes by the name of Sean Kilpatrick these days"

"I'd hate to think that this guy's only real sin is that he happens to look like me. Well, I guess we better get going. You can tell me more about him on the way."

They started to walk out of the office and Jack paused. "How about requesting some protection for him and his family if he has any?"

Agent Schroeder had a sinking feeling in his stomach. "The best I can do is call the locals and see if they'll cruise by more often. Since there's been no threat, expressed or implied, the FBI won't sanction it."

Jack was feeling more than just a little helpless. "I'm afraid when it comes to Michael, Sean whatever he calls himself, he doesn't threaten. He just does."

Jack and Agent Schroeder pulled into the job site twenty-five minutes later. They entered the mobile office and Nick stood to greet them. "Oh, Agent Schroeder you're back again. What can I do for you this time?" He extended his hand and they shook. Then Jack stepped out from behind Schroeder. Nick's head snapped in Jack's direction. "Dave I thought.... Son of a bitch, you could pass for Dave's double."

"That's what I've been told; also, that's who we are here to see. Could you ask him to come in here?" Jack said, still uncomfortable with his new dilemma.

Nick spoke as he tried not to stare at Jack. "Wish I could gentlemen, but he had to leave on a family emergency. His daughter's car broke down on the freeway. He left about an hour ago. Is there anything else I can do for you?"

Jack decided to take a seat to let Agent Schroeder handle any questions he felt he needed to ask. This was not his domain anymore and he did not wish to step on any toes unnecessarily.

Agent Schroeder had a gut feeling Ramón was more of a key to this investigation than Dave. He figured Nick would have the information they needed. "I was wondering if that Hispanic kid ever showed back up."

Nick picked up some envelopes from the desk. "No, I haven't seen hide nor hair of him since the day you first showed up here. I held onto his final paycheck for a couple of days hoping he'd show so I could give you a call, but nothing. We finally had to mail it out. It came back in yesterday's morning mail 'Incomplete or Unknown Addressee'. I asked some of the guys on the job site if they had seen him around here, or at some of the local hangouts. He used to frequent some topless joint downtown at lunchtime with some of the guys, but they've not seen him either. I even called his uncle. He told me the kid never stayed at a job long. He had hoped this time was going to be different because this was the longest he had ever held a job. He told me to mail the check to him and he'd make sure he'd get it. I told him I didn't think legally I could do that."

As Schroeder tried to think of another possible way to locate Ramón, he said, "We also checked out the address. It was bogus. No one there had ever heard of him. Could I have the information on this uncle?"

Nick wandered over to Grace's desk and picked up the Rolodex, thumbing through it to find a card. "Yeah sure. I'll scribble it down for you. Wish Grace was here then I'd have her print it out. It's hell on me when she calls in sick. I apologize for not giving it to you the last time you were here. It didn't even occur to me until the shipment came in this morning."

Nick wrote down the information on a piece of paper then handed it to Agent Schroeder. Schroeder did not get the connection between Ramón and the shipment.

"Shipment, what does that have to do with the kid?"

Nick did his best to explain the situation, "The kid was part of a package deal. His uncle owns the company that contracted the plumbing supplies. I always need general laborers so I agreed to hire the kid as a package deal. When the truck came in this morning, I thought I'd give him a call to thank him for finally being on time with this last shipment and asked if he had heard from the kid. I wish I could be of more help to you, but that's all I can think of right now."

With this information, Schroeder planed his next move. "No, you've been extremely helpful. We'll go wait at Mr. Martin's house. Maybe he can think of something that will help us locate either one of these guys."

Nick glanced over to where Jack was sitting, twirling a cigarette between his fingers. The resemblance spooked him. "What's the deal with your partner and Dave? Is there some connection?"

Schroeder also glanced over in Jack's direction. "Nick, that's a very good question. To be truthful, I don't exactly know."

As they were leaving, Jack stopped to ask Nick one more question. "Does Mr. Martin have a cell phone?"

Nick did not have to look this one up in the rolodex. "As a matter of fact he does? It's 951-555-2343."

Schroeder thanked him for his co-operation while Jack wrote down the number on the back of a business card he took from Grace's desk, and then placed it in the sleeve of his cigarette pack. At the same time, he took the cigarette he had been playing with and placed it back into the pack which he returned to his inside jacket pocket. They both climbed into a white sedan.

Schroeder was glad he did not light up. "Did you quit then pick up a new nervous habit?"

Jack fastened his seat belt. "No. I still smoke on occasions, usually on a stake out. I use to watch McCarron as he sat at the bar. He would drink whiskey shot after whiskey shot. He'd down more booze than most men could tolerate. Yet his speech would not slur, his walk would not stagger, and he would never miss a beat twirling his cigarette. He didn't drop it, he didn't break it, and he didn't smoke it until he walked out of the bar. All I could figure out was it was some sort of timing device for him. When it became more difficult, took more concentration to twirl it, it was time to stop drinking and go home. I never once saw him drunk, and I watched him for months. You know he's a hard one to figure, and I can't identify with him at all. One thing I do know, he is focused. Whatever he is planning on doing, he will do it, and God help anyone who gets in his way."

Agent Schroeder picked up his cell phone. "Give me the card with Martin's number."

Jack removed the card and handed it to him. "Not many things spook me, but knowing I'm about to meet my twin for a lack of a better word kind of unnerves me."

Schroeder pressed a button on the phone to hear a dial tone. "Yeah, I can only imagine. Guess I should warn him. Let him have a moment or two to adjust to the idea himself. Thanks for staying in the background."

Jack knew exactly what he meant. "I only did what I would hope someone would have done for me. Besides, I'm only along for the ride. Right?"

Schroeder started up the car. "Yeah right. Let's just hope the ride doesn't get too bumpy."

The Drop

On the way to Dave's house, Agent Schroeder stopped at a local taco stand and treated Jack to some ethnic food. As they sat in front of Dave's house, in a middle class section of Rancho Cucamonga, Jack took out the cigarette and began twirling it. They waited until almost 6 PM before the first car pulled up into the driveway. Alicen exited her '89 Toyota Corolla with a couple of grocery bags. She walked over to the white sedan and Jack was first to greet her. She almost dropped the two bags of groceries she was toting. "Wow, Daddy told me about you, but I didn't think you'd look **so much** like him. Um, my dad stopped by to pick up a couple of pizzas. He should be here any minute. Would you like to come in and wait?"

Jack held out his hand to take her bags. "That would be fine miss. I'm sorry I startled you." Jack carried the groceries and they went into the house.

Agent Schroeder stayed behind to call dispatch. As he prepared to join the others, Dave drove his truck into the driveway. With three pizza boxes in hand, he walked over to Agent Schroeder. He tried to extend his hand out from under the boxes to shake hands. "I apologize for being so late. It took forever for the tow truck to arrive. Then we had a heck of a time locating the part we needed to fix Alicen's car. Fortunately it was an easy fix. Where's my double you were telling me about?"

Schroeder, deciding he wanted to talk to Dave away from the ears of his daughter, placed his hand on Dave's arm. "I think you need to know that Detective Richardson is close to being a dead ringer for you, Dave. He's paler and has different mannerisms than you, but the resemblance is uncanny. He believes because of this likeness and Sean's psychological profile, it is highly possible that you and your family could be in harm's way. I tend to agree with him. I have requested additional police patrol from the local department here, but personally, I don't know how much good that will do. Do you have family, or friends you all could stay with while this investigation is pending?"

Dave concerned for the safety of his daughter began searching his mind for places they could go. "My parents have been deceased for a long time. Most of the people I would trust, I work with. If this Sean knows where I live, would it not be logical he would also know where my co-workers live?"

Schroeder sighed, "It's possible, but at least he'd have to search you out. That could buy us time. Can't you think of anyone else that could put you up for awhile?"

Dave stared down at the ground deep in thought. "Maybe someone from church. I can make some calls…Oh my God, what about Laura? He really had a thing for Laura."

Schroeder ready for any inquiries regarding Laura responded, "I've already taken care of that. I called in for additional patrol at her house. I don't think he'll go after her. I believe because of your likeness to Detective Richardson you would be the more likely candidate, especially since he displayed such hostility and contempt towards you…come on. Let's go inside before this pizza is stone cold."

Alicen was in the kitchen busily filling glasses with ice for the cola she had bought at the store. Jack was nervously waiting to finally meet his twin. He sat down at the dinning room table and continued to twirl the cigarette with his right hand. Dave and Agent Schroeder entered the house. As Dave set the pizza on the dinning room table, he just about lost his breath. Jack snapped the cigarette in half as he gazed upon his double. Dave stood still in shock. "Son of a bitch, I just figured it was other people's perception of us looking alike."

Jack deciding more drastic action was necessary, turned to Schroeder, "I think we should camp out here until we can get these people relocated." Then he questioned Dave, "Alicen says there's another daughter. Where is she?"

Dave finally regaining his composure, replied, "Trisha is living on campus at a college in Iowa. I don't think she'd be in any danger, do you? Do you know how weird this is to have my own image staring back at me?"

Agent Schroeder interjected with his decision on the matter, "We will definitely stay here tonight. I'll call it in. Where's your phone?" Dave pointed to the wall phone in the kitchen.

Alicen entered the room and placed four glasses of soda, paper plates, and napkins on the table. She opened the top of the box, removed three pieces of pizza, and placed them on a paper plate. "Dad, I'm scared. Should I go to Amy's house?"

Dave placed his arm around her, "It's going to be okay hon, it's going to be okay. I would rather we stay together. I'll call Ed and see if he knows of a place to stay. Otherwise we can go to a hotel, maybe down near Disney Land. Yeah, the Disney Land Hotel, it's big, it's always crowded and it's away from here. I'll have Laura and Matt stay with us. We could all be together. Would you like that?"

Alicen leaned her head into her Dad's shoulder, " Yeah, I'd like that. Anyplace would be better than here right now. Should I call Matt and Laura?"

Dave gently stroked his daughter's hair, "No hon, I'll call. They may detect the panic and fear in your voice. We need to stay calm. This Sean character may not even be someone we need to be concerned about. We are just taking precautions. Okay?"

Alicen feeling calmer bit off a piece of pizza to find it was stone cold. "Okay. Oh, gross. Let me heat this up." She packed up the pizza, box and all and placed it the oven. Dave disappeared into his bedroom to make the call.

A few moments later, he came back out with a concerned look on his face. "I forgot, Laura has class tonight and Matt must be working. No one answered. I left a message for them to call me." He sat down at the dinning room table and stared across at his mirror image twirling a cigarette between his fingers.

***

Sean and Ramón had cleaned out and abandoned the small house in Rubidoux. They had located a vacant warehouse off University Avenue in Riverside. It was near the Metro Link station. Sean had broken off one of the locks to a garage door. The Super Bee was now hidden from public view. They walked over to a theater complex nearby, bought their tickets and entered inside. The movie was unimportant. They just needed to waste some time until they figured the guard was settled in and comfortable. Ramón had overheard Nick complaining the security guard had been found sleeping on several occasions. They were hoping tonight would be one of his sleepy nights. This way they could have the advantage.

It was almost 10 o'clock when the movie let out. They took the Super Bee and headed towards the job site in Moreno Valley. Sean parked the car on the backside of the housing development. He and Ramón quietly yet quickly ran up to the back fence. Ramón removed a bag containing a half-pound of hamburger from a duffle bag and prepared to throw it over the fence. "Are you sure we put enough poison in this? I hate dogs and I hate dog bites."

Sean grabbed the bag from Ramón with disgust, "There's no poison in the meat. I put a Quaalude in it. I don't want to kill the dog. I just want him to sleep real hard for a while. Just long enough for us to get the job done."

The guard dog could be heard barking in the distance. Sean lobbed the bag over the fence and they both ran back about twenty yards from the fence perimeter. Serge ran and jumped at the fence barking into the darkness. Sean and Ramón laid still on the ground in the cold dark air.

The German Shepherd determining no threat was imminent sniffed the ground locating the hamburger. He tore open the bag and proceeded to eat his find in three bites. The security guard had been running up the hill finally to catch up with his loyal companion. Out of breath, he queried Serge, "Hey, what you got their champ?" He picked up the fast food bag to look at its contents.

"Damn kids throwing their trash over here. Come on. You know you're not supposed to eat this stuff. I feed you only the best, yet every time I turn around your digging into some trash. What am I going to do with you?"

The guard stuffed the empty bag into his coat pocket. The dog jumped up and nipped at his pocket. He swatted him away. As he walked past a trash bin, he threw it over.

"There we'll have no more garbage food tonight."

A few minutes later both dog and guard were back to the guard shack. Serge immediately laid down at his feet.

Sean and Ramón waited for a good half hour before they scaled the fence. Standing still on the other side of the fence, they listened. No barking. It appeared the coast was clear. They pulled dark colored stockings down over their faces and ran down to a partitioned area where supplies were stored. Sean removed a large pair of heavy-duty wire clippers from his utility belt. He cut the links in the fence to allow them access. Inside they located wooden crates labeled 'commode' with a small penlight. After prying open the first crate, they removed the wood shavings from the bowl and tank to reveal brick shaped items. They were airtight, sealed in plastic, and wrapped in ammonia-scented paper. Sean pierced through its protective envelope to expose the white powder with his knife. Taking his finger, he dipped it into the white substance, and then rubbed his finger against his gums.

"This is good stuff. Your uncle is all right. We'll make a fortune on this. Well, what are you waiting for, start loading up your duffle bag." Sean actually sounded giddy.

Ramón tackled the next crate with a crow bar. It easily opened and then he removed its contents into his bag. They continued this process repeatedly until his bag was nearly full.

The security guard's watch beeped. He laid down the newspaper and picked up his clipboard, writing down the time as he prepared for his rounds. "Come on Serge, it's time to go to work." The guard dog did not respond. He kneeled down and shook Serge. "Come on old dog, wake up." He could tell Serge was still breathing; he was just not getting a response. "Ah shit." The guard spat, suspecting fowl play. So he unfastened the small strap to his gun holster, and then proceeded up the hill where the dog had found the meat. Looking out into the dark, he could see a faint outline of a car parked just on the edge of the hill. Flashlight in hand he trekked down to the supply area. There he discovered a hole in the fence. He stood quietly to listen.

Sean was almost done removing the last of the bricks when a bright light was shone in his face. A voice bellowed out from behind the light. "Can I help you find something, boy? Or did you think this was just a good place to have a picnic?"

Sean squinted past the light to see a 9 mm staring back at him. In a louder than normal voice Sean spoke to him, "Old man, I think you better put that gun back in its holster and walk away, if you want to live."

With a puzzled expression on the guard's face he sarcastically said, "Well, asshole, it appears to me that I'm the one holding the gun. Therefore, I tell you what to do. Now, put your hands above your head very slowly..."

At this point, the guard heard the click of a gun's trigger being pulled back. He felt the cold barrel against his right temple. Ramón high on coke and the power over this man's life spoke in a very commanding voice.

"I think not ASSHOLE. Now put the safety back on and place the gun on the ground. DO IT if *you* want to live!"

Ramón's eyes were more intense than Sean had ever seen. The guard complied. As soon as he did, Sean seized a roll of duct tape from his bag and tied him up hog style. The old man lay prone in the dirt. Ramón screwed a silencer to the end of the barrel.

"He knows what you look like." He said as he placed the gun to the back of the guard's head. The guard closed his eyes as tight as he could. Ramón pulled the trigger. Blood splattered back on him then poured out onto the ground. The guard's body jerked momentarily then went limp. Ramón watched with fascination. "Cool."

Sean picked up his duffle bag and slung it over his shoulder. His steely blue eyes pierced right through Ramón.

"Great. Now they'll probably have every cop in the state out looking for us and we'll have to sit on the product til' things cool off. You just couldn't leave well enough alone could you? It's dark. I'm wearing panty hose over my head. What was he going to identify, a guy wearing all black, squatting in the dirt with a flat nose and big lips? Go get your bag. Let's get the hell out of here."

Ramón confused by Sean's response whined, "I thought I was protecting you, man."

Sean snapped back at him, "Just go get the duffle bag." Then he mumbled, "Now we need insurance."

Sean opened the trunk of the car. He removed the partition to expose the spare tire. He took a chain from his pant pocket, attached it to a hook located on the metal plating that the tire was sitting on. He pulled up on the chain and hooked it on another hook located near the back of the trunk. The tire lifted up to reveal a hidden compartment, which slid all the way under the car. They emptied the contents of the duffle bags into the compartment. He replaced the trap door, then the partition back over the spare tire.

"Come on. We have an errand to run."

They drove in an eerie silence. Sean turned down Dave's road. There he noticed a white sedan parked out front. Slowly, he passed by the house trying to see in a window. He could see two male shapes sitting at a table. Calmly and deliberately, he continued down the road. A patrol car passed them coming from the opposite direction. Ramón's body tensed up. Sean stared at the road ahead as though the patrol car did not exist. Plan A scratched, Sean prepared to carry out the contingency plan.

Laura's class had let out late. The professor had gone off on a tangent, regaling a story of his last trip to Paris. The only thing his story had lacked was slides of his tour of the Louvre. The last thing she wanted to do was run errands this late at night. Unfortunately, she couldn't fathom the idea of no coffee in the morning. So, this time she justified it as a necessity. After finding an all night market to pick up coffee, creamer, milk, bread, and eggs, she pulled into the driveway. The carport was dark. Laura exclaimed, "Damn, Matt forgot to leave the light on!" Turning the car off, she exited with her purse and keys in hand, locking the driver's door behind her. Quickly she opened the trunk to remove the bag of groceries. As she bent over to pick up the bag she heard a car behind her. Thinking it must have stopped at the neighbor's house, she continued getting her groceries. Just as she was about to close the trunk, a hand holding a damp cloth wrapped around her face covering her mouth and nose. Another arm tightly seized her around her waist and pulled her backward. A paralyzing fear pulsed through her body. She desperately tried to regain her balance to no avail. Her unseen mugger overpowered her and continued to pull her backward. The odor on the cloth started to make her woozy. With one final effort, she took a deep breath to scream. Her body fell limp.

Ramón dragged her limp body to the edge of the driveway where Sean had backed up the car. He opened the door, setting himself on the back seat. Then pushing himself back into the car with his legs pressed against the car floor and door jam, he dragged Laura's body in with him. As soon as her body was inside the car, Sean took off. The car door slammed shut due to the force of the forward momentum. Ramón continued to hold the cloth over her face. He rolled down the window a bit to abate the fumes rising from the cloth.

"Damn, this shit is strong."

Sean drove towards the freeway making sure he complied with the traffic laws, stopping at the intersection. The signal changed and Sean calmly turned onto the 10 freeway on ramp. He twisted his head around to make sure Ramón was keeping proper care of their insurance.

"Just keep that cloth over her face. The last thing we need is for her to wake up and start screaming."

Ramón held Laura's head in his lap with the cloth in place. He lifted his face to the open window to breathe in the fresh air. They drove on for a few more minutes then Sean turned off on the University Ave ramp.

As they pulled up in front of the warehouse, Sean instructed Ramón as to their next course of action. "We'll pick up our supplies then we're out of here."

Ramón peered down at the limp body. "What are we going to do with her?"

"Ah duh, moron. She comes with us."

Pulling on the emergency brake, he then exited the car while it was still running. He pulled open the garage door, and then jumped back into the car to bring it inside. Closing the door behind them, he took the key to open the trunk to allow a dim light to come from the trunk interior.

"Let's get her in the other room."

Ramón slid out from under Laura's head. He lifted her up by wrapping his arms around her chest area. Dragging her out to the garage floor, Sean grabbed her legs. They carried her to a small storage room off the garage.

The room had one small window at the top of the back wall, which Sean had Ramón paint black. Once inside, with the door closed, Sean hit the light switch. One stark bulb lit the room. They carried her limp body over and laid her against some duffle bags. The bags were now filled with clothing and miscellaneous supplies for their trip to Chicago. Sean took out his duct tape, and taped Laura's mouth, hands, and feet.

"That should keep her. Ramón, give me the keys to the truck."

Ramón dug into his pant pocket, retrieving the keys. He threw them and Sean snatched them from the air.

"I have to run a few errands. I need you to get all this stuff together, and then start loading the car."

Earlier Agent Schroeder had requested a patrol car be sent to the job site per Jack's request. They didn't know exactly how or why the location was important; it just seemed to be a focal point. Agent Schroeder sat in the living room staring at the TV with the volume so low it could not be heard. Jack, Dave, and Alicen were playing poker at the dinning room table. Periodically, Dave would pick up the portable and dial Laura's house.

"Still no answer. Someone has to be home soon. Maybe she went..." Dave started to say as the phone rang. He snatched the phone up off the table pressing the receive button.

"Hello, Laura.... Oh, yes, he is. Hold on a moment. Agent Schroeder it's for you."

Schroeder walked over taking the phone from Dave. With phone in hand, he walked into the kitchen just out of earshot of the three. It seemed as though the world stood still for those next few minutes until he came back into the room.

"We've got a problem. The officer that was dispatched to the job site located the security guard. He was bound and gagged then shot through the back of the head. It appears he interrupted them while they were retrieving a coke shipment. A few bricks of the stuff were found on the ground near a crate. I have asked for an officer to wait at Ms. Daniel's house. What kind of cars do they drive?"

Alicen reached over to grab hold of her father's hand. Dave squeezed her hand then gave the agent his information. "Laura drives a dark green Hyundai Elantra and Matt an 88 white Honda CRX."

Schroeder repeated the information back into the phone. He disconnected the call and placed the phone back on the table next to Dave.

"They will call me back as soon as a patrol car is in place."

Alicen with tears in her eyes tried to speak without crying, "Daddy, I'm so scared. What if something happened to Matt and Laura? What if…" She started to sob at the thought.

Dave patted her hand. Then he took his hand and gently lifted her face to make her look directly at him. "Don't do the 'What if' game. Don't start playing the worst-case scenarios in your head. We have to be strong. We have to believe and trust that God will protect them. It's out of our hands. Come on let's go sit on the couch."

As they got up to leave the table, the phone rang again. This time Dave just handed it to Agent Schroeder. "Schroeder here. Yes,…I understand. You searched the house?…Ah huh…Okay… Yeah, I've got it.… No, bring young Daniels here…about a half hour? Okay. No, I have no objections to having patrol cars parked out front here too. Yeah, I'll call for a tap on the line." He dialed the phone as he walked back into the kitchen area. A minute later, he returned to three anxious faces waiting for the update.

"The officer arrived at the house to find Ms. Daniel's car in the driveway. The trunk was left open and a bag of groceries and her glasses were found on the ground next to the car. Her son arrived as the officer was calling it in. He and the officer searched the house for Ms. Daniels, but did not locate her. At this point, I think we can assume she has been kidnapped. They are bringing someone in to dust for possible prints on her vehicle. We will maintain a patrol car in front of her house as well as here. There is an all points bulletin out. If they are out there, we are going to do our best to locate them. Ms. Martin, the Rialto Police are escorting your fiancée to this location. Jack, can I talk to you in the other room?"

Dave and Alicen situated themselves on the couch in the family room. Jack and Agent Schroeder secluded themselves away from them. Schroeder inquired, "Jack, no one appears to have seen anything at the Daniel's house. We don't even have a possible description on the vehicle. I was just wondering if this Sean has a particular M. O. regarding the types of vehicles he prefers? We know they would come and go on the job site in an old pickup truck, but it seems unlikely they would use this as a get away vehicle. Can you think of anything that might help us here?"

Jack paused for a moment, remembering the days when he watched Sean's every move.

"He was always fixing up these old muscle cars. He had an old Chevy Chavelle SS that he had restored when he left Buffalo. Guess he wanted something he figured could out run the police. My best guess would be he has another old muscle car."

Schroeder opened the line on the portable. "Thanks Jack." He then called dispatch so he could include this information in their all point's bulletin. Now was the hard part, waiting for a break. Waiting for any news, which would lead them to Sean and Ramón before any harm had come to Laura.

As Matt entered the house Alicen ran to him. She held him so tight he could hardly breathe. With tears in her eyes she lamented, "I'm so sorry about your Mom. They said they are doing everything possible to locate her. God I hope she's okay." She began sobbing into his chest.

Matt held her head pressed against his chest. "Me too." His voice faltered.

Dave sat on the couch with head in his hands, overwhelmed with the emotional turmoil welling inside him and with the turmoil taking place in his own home. Two patrol cars pulled up outside and then more FBI agents arrived to install the wiretap, but before the task was done, the phone rang. Agent Schroeder answered, "Hello?...Richardson it's for you." He cupped his hand over the receiver. "I think it's him. Try to keep him on the line until we have the tap going. We might get lucky."

Jack spoke into the phone, "This is Richardson."

Sean had driven down the freeway about 5 miles to use a pay phone with a previously purchased phone card. He very calmly and deliberately stated his message. "Now listen to me real good Richardson, because I will not repeat myself. I've got your woman and if you ever want to see her alive…"

Richardson interrupted, "What are you talking about my woman? You have Martin's woman. Have you completely lost it, or what McCarron?"

Sean snapped back, "Don't fuck with me, Richardson. You're not smart enough to fuck with me. You tried and what did it cost you. You lost that cop in the warehouse blast and your prime witness against me; well we all know what happened to her now, don't we. If you don't want this pretty little lady of yours to end up the same way, you'll make sure all your cop buddies give me a wide berth. You tell them if a cop car even comes close to me, I'll kill her. Oh, by the way, if you think she's expendable, I'll just have my man in Iowa pick up that sweet little thing out at the dorms. She's more my type anyway. You have 20 minutes to call off the dogs. Sorry, times up. No, trace this time." Sean ended sarcastically.

The phone went dead. Richardson looked over to where the agents had been setting up their equipment. Their eyes met his and they shook their head no. He placed the phone back down on the receiver. His heart was racing as he proceeded to notify everyone of the news.

"I'm very, very sad to report to you that Sean does have Laura. I don't want to give you any sense of false hope so I'm just going to tell it like I see it. Sean will only keep her alive as long as he sees a use for her. If he gets away, if he feels he has found a safe haven, Laura won't have a snowball's chance in hell of making it through this. I'm real sorry. If I was a praying man, I'd be begging for someone to see him before he leaves the state." Richardson gave them his version of the short and ugly as he liked to call it.

At the cinema complex, Sean eased the truck between a van and a pickup with a camper shell. The last show of the evening was about to begin. He believed the truck would be less conspicuous left there. Besides, the area was not very well lit. He climbed out of the truck and made his way back over to the warehouse. People were coming and going, so one more body walking through the parking lot would not be anything out of the ordinary. He went unnoticed.

Deciding to sneak up on Ramón, he chose not to go through the garage. Instead, he used a door under a stairwell where earlier he had picked the lock. Ramón could not be trusted. Ramón liked coke way too much. He was known for partying hearty on the mob's money, on the mob's dope. He was not going to let Ramón have more than his fair share of nothing. Weaving himself through the dark building, he came up to the door of the small room where Laura was being held. He could hear voices on the other side.

"Come on baby, you know your goin' to love this."

Sean ever so slowly, ever so quietly, opened the door just enough to see Ramón crouched over Laura where she was still bound and gagged. Ramón had his .380 semi automatic outfitted with a silencer and was running the barrel up Laura's inner thigh. He took his free hand and placed it in an opened bag of coke then he pulled out a hand full of coke and thrust it under her nose. "Sex, drugs, and violence, isn't that what it's all about?" Laura turned her head to avoid breathing in the white powder.

Sean stepped into the room. With disgust in his voice he commanded, "Put that shit away. That's not for your own personal use, asshole."

Ramón spun around, white powder flying everywhere, including Laura's face. "Damn it Sean, you scared the shit out of me. Someone could have gotten shot."

Sean cocked his head to one side. "Now there's an idea." As Sean walked over to Ramón, Laura tried to see who this second person was.

The coke was still burning her eyes and she had not seen her glasses since she was in the driveway at her house. Squinting her eyes, Laura tried to bring his image in more clearly. A wave of panic struck her as she realized who it was standing before her. This was the face of evil from the dance hall.

Sean did not speak to her, or acknowledge her presence. He was consumed with anger at Ramón wasting their profits. He was going to put a stop to it once and for all. In the most amicable voice he could muster up he stated, "Ramón since you couldn't be a good little boy and stay out of the candy, I'm afraid I'm going to need you to hand over your gun."

Ramón pulled his hand with the gun behind his back like a little boy caught doing wrong. "Why?"

Sean patiently held out his hand. In a kind, soft voice he said, "You're all doped up, Ramón. I can't let you accidentally shoot our insurance. You're so numbed, you probably wouldn't even know if you shot your own foot off. I can't let that happen to you buddy. I'm doing this for your own good. You know I've always watched out for you. You may not have liked the way I did it, but I always did it for your own good, didn't I?"

Hesitantly Ramón handed over his weapon like an obedient child. "Yeah, you got me out of trouble more times than I can count. Here."

Sean grasped the gun, released the safety, and then honed down right between Ramón's eyes. Ramón backed up flailing his hands in front of him. "Hey, what…th?" Sean fired, hitting his mark. Ramón fell to the ground with his eyes still open. Eyes that glared back at Sean in terror and disbelief. Blood oozed out onto the floor traveling towards Laura's leg. She had already scooted to the furthest corner of the room. There was nowhere left to go. Sean placed the gun in Ramón's hand, squeezing his fingers around the butt of the gun with a finger on the trigger. Still holding Ramón's hand on the gun, he lifted his other hand and made it hold the barrel, pointing it at the bullet entry wound. Then he allowed Ramón's hand and the gun to drop to the floor. He removed the clip out of the gun, removed the bullets, and then placed the clip back. Sean looked up to see Laura cuddled in the corner. Their eyes meet. His eyes were cold and calculating, but he did not speak a word to her.

Sean unzipped Ramón's bag to find a couple bricks of coke stashed inside. "I knew the asshole was ripping me off. Serves him right." He said looking down at Ramón's lifeless body. He placed the coke in his own bag. Taking his bag and a brief case, he left the room, turning out the light as he did. Laura frozen with fear, sat on the cold floor unable to move, unable to scream. She could feel Ramón's blood hit her leg, but she was now unable to tell which way she should move to avoid it. In the darkness, she prayed for God's mercy. She prayed the face of evil would not return.

It was around 3 AM and Detective Richardson had wandered outside to smoke a cigarette. He made small talk with the patrolmen stationed at the Martin house. If there were two things he hated it was the sense of powerlessness and helplessness. Right now, he was overwhelmed with both. He took long deliberate drags off the lit cigarette.

"So, how long have you been on the force?"

The officer leaned on his patrol car while he talked with Jack. The window was rolled down so he could hear the radio calls as they came in. "It'll be five years this October. My wife hates it when I pull this shift. I can't say that I blame her."

Jack threw his finished cigarette on the ground. "Yeah, I know police work is hard on marriages."

The radio inside the patrolmen's car squawked, "185, CHP has just reported the possible 207 suspect traveling north bound on the 15 freeway just past the 10 intersect heading towards Victorville in a late 60's Chevy Chavelle SS, or Dodge Super Bee, gray, plate number 3AJC467. The Department Of Motor Vehicles shows these plates belong to a 98 Nissan 4 door. Suspect appears to be alone in the vehicle. They have two units in pursuit code 2 keeping their distance at visual. Current pace speed 65 miles per hour. We have a helicopter on route for high altitude observation. CHP is requesting the FBI to advise on a code 100 to be set up before Apple Valley with permission to use road tacks."

The patrolman had reached inside his patrol car and retrieved the hand mic. He replied, "185, ten-four. 1023 while I relay the information to the FBI on location." The patrolman turned to Richardson. "What'd you think? Is this your guy? Doesn't sound like he has the woman? That could be bad, very bad news."

Richardson lit up another cigarette. "It's him and he's got her all right. I'd bet a month's pay he's got her with him. Where's the 15 freeway from here?"

The patrolman moved away from his vehicle. "Before I give you directions so you can go off on your own pursuit, I think I'll relay this information to Agent Schroeder."

The officer and Richardson went inside the Martin house. The patrolman relayed the dispatchers report to Schroeder away from listening ears in the other room. Before Schroeder had time to respond, Jack piped in, "I know we don't even have confirmation yet that this is Sean, but I know it's him. I feel it in my gut. Time is of the essence here. The longer we wait the further away he'll be. If they end up cornering this guy, there is only one person he will negotiate with and that's me. You know it. We have got to get on the road now. That way I'm there to deal with this scum and hopefully save this woman's life. These good people here will still have the other agents and the patrolmen in the event this is a wild goose chase. Come on Schroeder what do you say?"

Schroeder toyed with the keys in his pant pocket. "Let me call it in."

Jack grabbed Schroeder by the back of the arm. "Screw policy and procedure. For once in your life go by the seat of your pants and just do what is right. Just do what needs to be done. You can call it in from the car."

They stood there staring at each other in a deafening silence, then Schroeder turned to the patrolman. "Tell dispatch to go ahead and set up the intercept and be ready with the road tacks as a last resort and that I'm on my way with the negotiator. Let's go Jack. It looks like we get the bumpy ride after all." Schroeder gave a nod to one of his fellow agents. "Davis you're in charge now."

The door slammed shut behind them. Dave had been in the bathroom splashing cold water on his face to help him stay awake while the three had been talking. At the sound of the door slamming, he exited to find out what all the commotion was about. He was wiping his face with a hand towel.

"What's going on? Was there some news?"

Agent Davis spoke to Dave in a calm and authoritative voice, "They are just going to check out a possible lead. They'll call if they find anything. Why don't you go rest?"

Dave looked out into the front room where Alicen had fallen asleep in Matt's arms. Raising his head from the arm of the couch, Matt stared back at Dave with sleepy eyes. He mouthed, "Any news?" Dave shook his head no then responded to Agent Davis, "There will be no rest until my Laura is back in my arms. No, there will be no rest."

The 15 freeway weaves through the desert with long dark stretches of road between on-off ramps, which become fewer and fewer the farther north one travels. The two highway patrolmen had been following Sean's car in what they considered a safe and inconspicuous distance for over ten minutes. Sean had increased the pace speed to about 85 miles per hour. As long as the pursuit remained on the freeway there was an element of control and confinement of a potentially dangerous situation.

Officer Daniel Hernandez was in the lead car. His radio squawked to inform him the helicopter was less than a minute away and the FBI with the negotiator were in route. He reached down to pick up his mic to acknowledge the call and for a moment took his eyes off the road. When he looked back at the road, Sean's car disappeared from sight.

"Shit. Where did he go?"

Hernandez turned off his headlights and pulled into the number three lane.

"Hank did you see where he went?" He said speaking into the mic.

Officer Hank Trask pulled into the number two lane. They both reduced their speed to 45 MPH in the event the suspect's vehicle had pulled over to the side of the road, waiting to see the vehicles behind him pass as to identify who had been following him. Officer Trask replied into his hand mic, "I saw him pull into the number three lane and then he was gone. I'll proceed ahead to Cleghorn as though I'm just doing a routine drive through. Hopefully, as I pass by him he'll pop back out."

Officer Trask proceeded ahead and Hernandez stopped on the shoulder of the road. The mic still in Hernandez's hand, he called it in. "8024 we have lost visual of the suspect going north on the 15 just past the Kenwood Avenue on-ramp. I am stationary on the shoulder with lights out. Eighty-twenty is proceeding north on 15 to Cleghorn Ave. Is AIR in position?"

Dispatch crackled back a response, "Ten four 8021 AIR83 is in position. Suspect's location is negative."

"Eighty-twenty-four, ten-four. I'll wait 2 minutes then proceed ahead."

"Ten four 8021."

Officer Trask continued up the road past the truck weigh station, trying not to be too conspicuous, as he did his best to locate the suspect's vehicle. He continued to the next off ramp to do a turn around, as though he was just cruising his section for possible violations.

As soon as the patrol car was committed to the southbound route, Sean poked his head out the window to listen. The sound of a train running through the pass could be heard as a distant rumble. He felt confident it was safe to continue on his journey. He pulled out of the weight station onto the freeway, turning his headlights back on. The helicopter hovering almost 2,000 feet above observed the movement and immediately contacted the pursuit vehicles.

"Eighty-twenty-one we have a lock on the suspects vehicle."

"Ten-four AIR83. I have visual."

Officer Hernandez also turned on his headlights. Sean was hyper aware of the movement around him, stepped on the gas pedal until it hit the floor. The car accelerated to 105 MPH. Sean had only moments to decide what he was going to do. He could continue on the 15 freeway and hope it was not a cop car behind him, or take the 138 heading towards Lancaster.

Lancaster was his old stomping ground. He lived there while in Junior High School before his parents had moved to San Diego. He still had friends there, friends who would not hesitate to hide him for a while.

The car behind him was still keeping a steady pace. He could see additional headlights coming up in line with the vehicle behind him. The probability was high. They had not shown their hand yet, but it seemed clear his only option was to try to outrun them on desert back roads.

Highway 138 came up fast and he almost missed the turnoff. The Super Bee fishtailed as he made his way off the main road. Dust and gravel kicked up a small dust cloud. As long as he could get through the first few miles of this highway with its hills and curves, he knew he could outrun most any car on the road. The rest of the highway was pretty much straight and with the full desert moon he could turn off the headlights again. He figured this would make it more difficult for his pursuers to see him in the event he had to make a quick turn onto a side road. Adrenaline was coursing through his body. The excitement of the chase, the excitement of out running, outsmarting the police was a game he always enjoyed. At this point, nothing mattered, but the game.

The air unit had successfully tracked Sean through the pass and was still locked on, even though no lights could be seen. Officer Trask and Hernandez had lost distance and sight of Sean's car. They had to rely on air support to give them updates. It was almost as though they were flying blind. Once Sean had hit the straightaway, he accelerated again to speeds well over 100 MPH, taking air when he would hit the dips in the road. Even though he had lost the headlights behind him, he knew they were not far behind. He also knew they would probably try to set up roadblocks ahead. He was playing the odds it would take more than twenty minutes for them to set up. In twenty minutes he would be on roads he knew better than any cop. In twenty minutes, he would be home free.

The old farm hand had driven his faithful stake bed to Pear Valley every morning at four AM to work the groves for the last twenty years. He had seldom met with any traffic at this time of the morning. Most of the time, he did not even bother to come to a complete stop at the stop sign before pulling out onto the main road. This morning was no exception. He slowed for a brief moment then pulled out onto the highway as he always did.

Sean had just come up over a small hill and could not see the lights of the truck until he was almost on top of him. He could not see past the truck to determine if there was any on coming traffic. His instinctual response was to slam on the brakes, so as not to crash into the backside of the truck and decapitate himself. As he did, his car spun out of control. After completing a three-sixty, his car slid off the shoulder. The brakes locked up and the momentum of the vehicle continued sideways through the sand until it finally was stopped by a telephone pole.

As the car hit the pole, Sean's lap belt broke way. His body was thrown with the motion of the car towards the pole. His shoulder hit the metal door. He could hear the bone snap. Then his arm met with the door. The bone shattered and forced its way to his rib cage. Sean could feel his ribs puncture his lungs. The passenger car door wrapped itself around the pole and Sean's head made contact with the window as it took the full impact of the telephone pole. The windshield cracked from right to left, as Sean lost consciousness. Blood ran out of his nose, mouth, and ears. His body lay still under the glow of the desert moon.

The old man confused by the sound of breaking glass and crunching metal behind him, pulled over to the side of the road, designed for slow vehicles. He climbed out of the cab of the truck to inspect the darkness. There he could see the gray Super Bee resting against the telephone pole. Steam from the radiator spewed out. Shuffling towards the vehicle to inspect the contents, he could see the lights of the patrol cars speeding towards him. At the same time a bright spotlight from the helicopter shone on the scene of the accident. Loud speakers bellowed from above scaring the old man half to death.

"Sir, step away from the vehicle. Officers are on their way."

As quickly as the old man could, he moved back over to his truck and waited for the patrol cars to get into position. Hernandez and Trask were the first to arrive. They parked the patrol cars in such a manner, if Sean's car were to try to leave the scene he would be trapped in. One car parked in front of Sean's car and the other to the back. They exited their vehicles with weapons drawn. Hernandez inched his way towards the disabled vehicle and yelled out, "Come out with your hands over your head."

The old man placed his hands over his head fearing the officers would think him somehow involved with this ominous steaming demon in the dark. There was no response. Officer Trask approached the rear of Sean's car with caution. The spotlight from above revealed a single body slumped to the side. Hernandez assessed, this one was not going anywhere fast, if he was going anywhere at all. He returned to his patrol car and picked up his mic to relay the current conditions.

"Eighty-twenty-four, we have a 1180 with a possible 1144. The suspect's vehicle is disabled."

Dispatch responded to the call. "Eighty-twenty, There is an ambulance and tow truck in route, ETA 10 minutes."

His patrol car radio piped up again. "Eighty-twenty-one, eighty-twenty, this is Agent Schroeder. Have you found the kidnap victim?"

Officer Trask spoke into his mic again, "The kidnap victim is not in sight."

Jack ripped the mic out of Schroeder's hand. "Have you checked the trunk of the car?"

Before either officer had the opportunity to respond, Schroeder's car came bounding over the slight incline in the road to rest in-between the two patrol cars. Jack raced out to make sure they indeed had been pursuing Sean. He approached the car with caution. Hernandez yelled out, "He's not going anywhere."

Sean's bloodied body laid limp against the passenger door. Jack reached in through the window to remove the keys from the ignition. His fingers grasped the keys and he struggled to remove them from the steering column. Suddenly, he felt a cold clammy hand grab him at his wrist. Sean's steely blue eyes met Jack's. He spoke in nearly an inaudible voice. "Help me." Jack stared into Sean's dying eyes. He snatched the keys and pulled his arm away from Sean's weak grasp. Sean's body again fell limp and still. As quickly as he could, Jack went to the trunk of the car. With the keys in hand, he fumbled through them, trying each one in the trunk lock. Hernandez positioned himself beside him. "I've got a good crow bar in the car if you can't get the lock to open...I presume that's your man?"

Jack now tried the next key in the lock. "Yep, that was him. I just hope he didn't take Ms. Daniel's down with..." The trunk opened and there he found Laura, still bound and gagged. Her body was resting against a duffle bag. The bricks of cocaine Ramón had absconded had been thrown in the back with her. As she had tried to loosen herself from her bindings, she had inadvertently kicked them open. Then, with the car being thrown around in the accident the white powder had flown around in the trunk and rested on her body. Her head and face had been knocked around pretty hard causing blood to stream down her face. The blood mixed with the white powder gave her face strange streaks of pink. Jack checked her pulse in her neck then gently removed the duct tape from her mouth. Concerned for her welfare Jack asked, "What's the ETA of the ambulance?"

Hernandez looked down at his watch. "About three minutes. Did you find a pulse?"

Jack removed a Swiss army knife out of his pocket, opened it, and proceeded to remove the tape from her hands and ankles. "Yeah, it's faint, but yeah."

Officer Hernandez concerned about Laura going into shock brought a blanket over from his car and handed it to Jack. Jack placed the blanket over her and softly whispered, "Come on Laura you can make it. We'll have you in a hospital in no time. Come on little lady wake up. Show us what you're made of." Jack removed a handkerchief from his pocket, wiped the blood mixed with the cocaine from her eyes and nose. Laura tried to open her eyes, but the cocaine caused them to sting and she was unable to focus. She coughed trying to expel the foreign substance from her lungs. Jack did his best to comfort her. He stroked her hair as he spoke, "That's it, fight. Fight for your life, little woman. You've people waiting for you at home."

Laura opened her eyes again and tried to look into Jacks eyes. Her voice was so weak as she spoke, Jack could barely hear her. "How did you find me? I knew you would. I prayed you would."

Jack was more than a little unnerved by Laura believing he was Dave, placed his finger on her lips to hush her. "Shh, save your energy."

She reached up and touched Jack's face. "Have I told you lately that I love you?"

Jack's eyes welled up with tears. Then Laura's eyes rolled back and her body started convulsing.

The next few minutes seemed like an eternity. The ambulance came. They said she had a weak yet rapid pulse. Her pupils were unresponsive. It appeared she had gone into a coma from a drug overdose. They were able to stabilize her then transport her to Loma Linda's trauma unit.

Loma Linda's emergency facilities were known for their excellent care of trauma patients. There she would have the best care anyone could ever hope to have. Dave and the rest of her family were also in route to the hospital. The next 48 hours were crucial. If she made it through the next two days, her chances looked good.

Bittersweet Tears

Dave was pacing up and down the hallways of the hospital, periodically checking into the nurse's station for a status report. Matt kept going to the pay phone to call his brother since his cell had no reception inside. He worried that Kyle had not kept his payments up and he was calling a disconnected number. Alicen returned from the vending machine for the third time with three more cups of coffee. As she entered the waiting room, Matt lifted his head out of his hands. She sat down next to him on the cold vinyl couch, placing the coffee on the table in front of them. Matt took the coffee cup from the table and rolled it in-between the palms of his hands.

"I called Jennifer, Mom's friend, to let her know what's going on. She should be here anytime. She was a blubbering, basket case. I've been calling Kyle once every ten minutes or so. God I hope he's getting his messages. I'd hate for him not to be here in the event Mom's condition gets worse. I don't think he'd ever forgive himself if..."

Matt tilted his head back taking a deep breath trying to keep a handle on his emotions. Alicen snuggled in closer to Matt. She patted his arm in an attempt to calm him down and then rested her head on his shoulder.

An overwhelming sense of longing to hold Laura in his arms filled every fiber of Dave's body. He felt the need to be near his loved ones and started to walk into the waiting room. Standing in doorway, he could see his daughter comforting Matt. He could not bring himself to enter the room to even retrieve his coffee. He left unnoticed. As he walked down the corridor, a door swung open. Bolting through the door, Jennifer rushed up to Dave. Without hesitation, she threw her arms around his neck, and started sobbing. Dave reciprocated, patting her on her back. "There's been no news. The doctors have been with her for almost an hour now. It's in God's hands now. I just really hope his says, yes, to my prayers."

Jennifer backed off from Dave's arms and took hold of his hand. She placed his hand to her tear stained cheek. "He has to, he just has to." Jennifer wrapped her arm around Dave and they moved toward the waiting room.

Dr. Prakash had worked the trauma unit for more than eight years. Still, he always found it difficult to talk to family members. He stood, still dressed in his surgery garb, at the nurse's station inquiring as to whom he needed to talk. The nurse pointed in the direction of Dave and Jennifer. He slowly, calmly, and deliberately, walked down the corridor to meet them. In a thick East Indian accent he asked, "Are you relatives of Ms. Martin?" Dave and Jennifer could not speak, but in unison shook their heads yes. "Are there more family members here? I'd like to talk to everyone at the same time." Dr Prakash continued. Dave was terrified to speak and when he finally got the words out his voice broke, "Yes, her son is in the waiting room."

"Good, let's go in there where we can have some privacy."

They all gathered in the small room and closed the door. Dr. Prakash proceeded to explain to them what Laura had gone through and what her chances might be. "Ms. Daniels is in critical condition. She is still comatose and we are having difficulty keeping her stable. This is due to the amount of cocaine in her system which causes her to continue to have convulsions. I don't know how much her heart can take. She appears to be a healthy woman, but there are other injuries. We can't fully determine the extent of the damage from these injuries until we have her stable enough to run some tests. I will tell you this, I don't believe she has any internal bleeding, but it is probable that there is spinal damage and a concussion."

Jennifer gasped, "Oh my God. Does that mean she will be paralyzed?"

Dr. Prakash continued, "At this point that's difficult to say. Right now, we are more concerned with her making it through the night. Right now she is literally fighting for her life, ma'am."

Dave's chest had tightened with fear. Finally, he remembered to breathe. He knew he needed to see her one more time, just in case it was the last time. He also felt in his inner most being if he could be with her, talk to her, she would come back to him. Desperately he pleaded, "Maybe, if we are able to talk to her, touch her, we could help her fight. She might respond to those who love her. When will we be able to see her?"

Dr. Prakash never prevented family and loved ones from being with a critically ill patient. He knew the power they could have on the possibility of patient's recovery. "We are having her moved to ICU as we speak. As soon as she is set up, providing there are no more complications, I will come out and bring you in to see her."

It was amazing how long thirty minutes could be. They all sat in the waiting room, silently staring at the floor. Detective Richardson had finally made it to the hospital after the arduous task of filling out reports. He awkwardly stood in the doorway of the waiting room. "Mr. Martin, could I speak with you out here, please."

Dave went with him down the hall, away from the others. Richardson stopped once he felt he was a comfortable distance away from the others. Jack's heart was racing. The palms of his hands were sweating as he told Dave what he knew needed to be said.

"I understand Laura is not doing well. I'm sorry. I...I wish there was something I could do, something I could have done to prevent this whole disaster. I wanted you to know that Sean died at the scene of the accident. He won't be hurting anyone again. The police found his truck at a movie theater and they are still looking for his partner. Um... I just wanted you to know that before Laura lost consciousness she spoke to me...well actually she thought I was you. I wanted you to know her last words were...her last words were, 'Have I told you lately that I love you?'"

Dave's eyes welled up with tears. "Thank you." He took a breath trying to regain his composure. Again, he said, "Thank you."

Jack stood in silence not knowing what to do, and then he finally said, "I just thought you'd needed to know." Then he left. There was nothing more for him to do.

Dr. Prakash returned to the waiting room. "Come on, it is time. We have her ready."

Dave stood next to the doctor, while Jennifer, Matt, and Alicen listened intently Dr. Prakash proceeded to tell them what they were about to see and experience. "Now let me tell you what to expect when you go into the room. We have many machines hooked up to her and tubes running from her body to these machines. Do not be afraid of these machines. It is important you know these machines are there to help Ms. Daniels. Do not show fear in your voices when you talk to her. You may think it foolish of me say these things, but I have found if the family shows fear and despair, the patient senses this and their recovery may be less than what we hope for. Do you understand what it is I am trying to tell you?"

The four of them nodded their heads yes.

In the room they all stood back away from Laura's bedside. Only the humming sounds of a machine could be heard. Dave was the first to go to Laura's bedside. He brushed her bloodied hair back from her forehead and kissed her ever so gently. He gently took her hand in his, making sure not to disturb the IV's and knelt on one knee at her bedside with her hand resting against his cheek. He bowed his head in prayer. When he was done, he lovingly gazed upon her face. Then in not quite a whispered tone he said, "I love you with every fiber of my being, I love you. You are the best thing that has ever happened to me and I want you to come back to me. I want you to grow old with me, to bounce our grand babies on our knees while we sit in that porch swing we've talked about. You've got to fight little girl, like you've never fought before. Matt, Alicen, Jennifer and I, we are all here for you, waiting for you to come back." Dave kissed her hand. Tears rolled down his cheeks and fell to the bedding below.

Matt mustered up all his strength to comfort Dave and express his heart felt love for his mother. He placed his left arm around Dave and his right hand on his mother's arm. Matt bent down and kissed his mother's cheek.

"Mom, it's Matt. You're safe now. You're in the hospital and nobody can hurt you. The doctors are doing everything in their power to make you well and right now God has a barrage of prayers being thrown at him. We need you to hang in there and fight the good fight. Please Mom, don't give up...I love you."

He leaned down over his mother's body and to the best of his ability, he hugged her through the medical equipment. Now, tears rolled down his cheeks. Turning away from Laura's bedside, he wiped them from his face. He stood in the middle of the room like a lost little boy. Alicen wrapped her arms around him and pulled him into her body. He sobbed, "It's so hard to see her like this." Alicen quickly escorted Matt out of the ICU room.

Jennifer had been standing against a wall. The tears had been rushing down her face as she stared at Laura's lifeless body and listened to Dave and Matt talk to her. She did not know if she could, but she knew she had to speak to Laura. She knew it could very well be her last chance. She hesitantly moved towards the bed. Dave noticed the difficulty she was having and moved away. Jennifer's whole body was trembling, as she pulled up a chair next to Laura's bed. She stroked Laura's cheek and moved in closer. She softly talked into her ear.

"Laura honey, this is Jen. You know, your pain in the butt friend? You've got to come back to us, sweetie. You're my best friend; my only friend, and I don't know what I'd do without you. You're the only one who tries to keep me on the straight and narrow. I swear girl, cross my heart I swear, you come back to us, I'll go to church every Sunday for the rest of my life. You hear that? You won. You've got to live just to see me keep my promise. Okay?" At this point, she buried her face in the pillow which Laura's head was resting on. "Please God don't let her die." She sobbed.

Dave placed his hand on Jennifer's shoulder. She did her best to compose her self. Large crocodile tears fell from her face, as she looked up with pleading eyes and asked, "Do you really believe God listens our prayers?"

Dave look over at Laura's lifeless body laying on the hospital bed, wondering if she was still really in there, then held Jennifer's chin in his hand. "I am certain he hears our prayers, Jen. He just doesn't always answer them in the way we would like him to."

***

The church was filled with the fragrance of red roses. Jennifer thought she had never seen so many roses in her entire life. Pastor Reeves had given a beautiful and touching service. At the podium, Dave removed a piece of paper from his coat pocket. He pressed on the paper to straighten it out and leaned forward to speak into the microphone.

"Thank you all..." The microphone let out a high pitch screech. He jumped back slightly and began again. "Thank you all for coming today. Today is, without a doubt, the most difficult day of my life. For today I must say Good-bye to the woman I love, my Laura." He reached into his jacket pocket to retrieve a pair of reading glasses and proceeded to read.

"When a man has a few close friends who are with him through thick and thin, he is blessed. When a man has children who teach him the true meaning of pure and innocent love, he is truly blessed. When a man has found his soul mate, a woman so special her mere presence brightens even the most dismal of days, his cup runneth over. This was my Laura. There wasn't a time, when she walked into the room that my heart didn't lighten up at the joy of seeing her. I think my most precious memory of our time together was the time I was showing her the construction site I was working on. The streetlights were not yet working and you could see the stars like sparkling little diamonds in the sky. I don't know what possessed me, but I took hold of her and we started dancing. We held each other close, went round and round in circles for the longest time. The thought of never being able to hold my Laura in my arms again leaves an emptiness in my heart. An emptiness that could only be comparable to the pit of hell. The only things I have left to cling to are the memories of our time together.

What I admired most about her was her desire to always do what was right. No matter how difficult, no matter what the cost to her own personal comfort, she sought to do what was right and honorable in the eyes of God. How blessed I was to know her, to love her, but most of all be loved by her. This brings me to a poem I wrote.

In my journey of life, I have traveled down many a road
 Had I the knowledge of the events to come,
had they been foretold
I would not have changed a single moment in time.

For it all led to the day My Laura I would find.

 With tears of joy, I greeted the birth of each of my daughters

With tears of gladness did I thank my heavenly father

Grace and mercy he has shown on a wretched sole like me.

He gave me a most incredible woman whom I could love.

Kissed by the angels, her smile sparkled like the night stars above.

Today as we lay her body to rest, tears of sadness fills my heart.

Her life abruptly taken from us, when I had hoped we would
never be apart.

Of all the tears my eyes have shed, with joy, gladness, and sorrow

Today my eyes weep that there will be no tomorrow

To look upon her loving face

To have the honor of her presence before me grace.

So now bittersweet tears roll down my cheek

For I know my Lord, her soul does keep

No more pain or sorrow does her sweet spirit know

For she basks in the glory of my Father's glow

Through bittersweet tears, I say good-bye

To meet again when I die."

Jennifer, Alicen, Trisha, and Matt sat on the front row bench grasping each others' hands as Dave read his poem. Jennifer wiped her eyes and nose. She peered over to where Kyle was sitting, alone and separate from the rest of them. He was slumped over in his seat with his head hanging down, staring at his feet.

Dave picked up his piece of paper, folded it, and placed it back in his jacket pocket. He walked over to the casket where Laura's body lay, reached back into his pocket, and pulled out a small box. He opened the box to view a diamond ring he had bought her. A tag attached to the ring with a short string read in small print, "The real thing for my real woman." After one last look, he closed the lid on the box and placed it by Laura's still hands. He returned to his seat, next to Kyle. They both stared blankly at the floor.

Pastor Reeves approached the podium to give the final instructions. "During the next fifteen minutes, those of you who would like to say one last good-bye will have the opportunity to do so. At 12:30 we will be traveling to the gravesite to lay this sweet soul in her final resting place. Those of you who would like to attend are welcome."

The sun was shinning brightly. The sky was clear and blue. A soft warm breeze wisped across their faces as they stood at the burial site. Pastor Reeves spoke his final words.

"The good book says our Lord knows the number of hairs on our head, he knows us while we are still in our mother's womb. He is aware of the sparrow when it falls to the ground and he knows the number of days of our life. With this in mind, we can be rest assured Laura is in the best of care. She now rests in the arms of the father where there are no more tears, no more sorrow, and no more pain. Glory, glory to God on high as we commit this soul to your care. May the Lord be merciful and kind to those she leaves behind."

Matt took his place at the head of the casket where the Pastor had just been standing. He had a guitar slung over his right arm and brought it into position to play. He strummed a few cords then began to sing.

"Amazing grace! (how sweet the sound) That sav'd a wretch like me! I once was lost, but now am found, Was blind, but now I see. Twas grace that taught my heart to fear, And grace my fears reliev'd."

Matt had done so well until this point. His voice faltered and failed all together. His chest heaved as he sobbed. Dave quickly pressed the play button on the cassette player and the same song echoed through the air. He walked over and placed his arm around Matt while he sobbed.

"You did real good, son. Your mother would have been proud of you."

As they lowered Laura's body into the ground, those who attended turned and walked away. All three of the girls were clinging on to each other as they made their way to the car. Matt and Dave also started to leave when Dave noticed Kyle still at the gravesite, staring at the ground beneath him. He came up beside him, and they both stood there watching as the dirt was being placed over the casket. Without looking up, Kyle spoke, "I can't remember the last time I told her I loved her. The last time we spoke, it was in anger. I said and did things I didn't mean and now I can't say...I can't tell her I'm sorry...I can't ask her to forgive me...I can't tell her how much she really meant to me...I can't thank her for loving me, for giving me life, a good life. I'll never be able to make it up to her."

Dave compassionately wrapped his arm around Kyle and pulled him close. "There is one thing you can do. You can live your life with honor, courage, and commitment to do what is right. It's never easy, but you know if you did what is right, Laura would be looking down at you with the biggest smile you could ever imagine. If you're willing to do the right thing, I think I could talk Nick into giving you your old job back. What do you think kiddo?"

For the first time Kyle looked into Dave's kind eyes. "I'd like that, thank you."

As they started to drive away from the cemetery, Alicen fished into her purse for a letter. "Oh Dad, I forgot to tell you. You got a letter from the Art Gallery."

Dave drove the car over to the side of the road so he could read the letter. He read it aloud.

"Dear Mr. Martin, The Logan Art Gallery is pleased to announce we will proudly be exhibiting Ms. Daniel's work the third week of October." Dave found he could not read on. The knot in his throat would barely allow him to speak. "It looks like Laura finally gets her art exhibit. My God, life sure does have its strange twists and turns."

Kyle choked out, "I guess that's why you wrote your poem, Bittersweet Tears."

Dave peered into his rear view mirror to see tears running down Kyle's face then with a kind and loving smile he spoke softly, "Yeah, I guess so."

THE END

Biography

I was born in Jamestown, New York and I am currently living in Southern California with my husband Doug, our dog, and two cats. In 1992 I started portrait drawings after having the misfortune of working in a bank that was held up twice in forty-five days. The second robbery was a violent takeover. My adventure in drawing was my way to keep in touch with those things in this world that make life worthwhile, those things that illustrate the glory of God. I began my pursuit of writing shortly after my father, Donald V. Gustafson, died. Here I found a way to express my emotions through various characters in this novel. Grieving is a process which is different for each individual who must labor through it. Whether I was faced with the grief of the loss of my security in the workplace, facing the terror of the possibility of the loss of my own life, or the actual loss of a loved one, I have chosen to take what I consider the most positive and constructive course toward my own healing, this being through painting and writing. I hope you have enjoyed the end product of my journey.